DEKOK AND THE
CORPSE AT THE CHURCH WALL

DeKok
and the
Corpse at the Church Wall

by

BAANTJER

translated from the Dutch by H.G. Smittenaar

INTERCONTINENTAL PUBLISHING

ISBN 1 881164 10 1

Printing History:
    1st Dutch printing: 1976
    2nd Dutch printing: 1978
    3rd Dutch printing: 1979
    4th Dutch printing: 1980
    5th Dutch printing: 1983
    6th Dutch printing: 1985
    7th Dutch printing: 1987
    8th Dutch printing: 1989
    9th Dutch printing: 1990
    10th Dutch printing: 1991
    11th Dutch printing: 1992
    12th Dutch printing: 1993

    1st American edition: 1994

Typography: Monica S. Rozier
Cover Photo: Peter Coene

DeKok
and the
Corpse at the Church Wall

1

Detective-Inspector DeKok of the Amsterdam Municipal Police (Homicide), attached to the ancient police station at Warmoes Street, at the edge of the Red Light District, pressed down on the door handle and hoisted his heavy body out of the police car. He slammed the door behind him, leaned against the car and looked up at the slender spire of the Old South Church. It was eleven minutes past nine. Underneath the large clock he could see the number 1614 in gold, sparkling in the sun. DeKok pushed his old, decrepit felt hat a little deeper over his eyes and grinned to himself. The old architects knew the true worth of their creations, knew they would survive the ages. That is why the *Anno Domino* was a sacred concept to them, worthy to be written in gold.

He detached himself from the car and ambled across the grass field, preceded by Vledder, his young assistant, partner and friend. They approached a number of uniformed constables, standing under a high, exquisitely detailed glass-in-lead window. One of them turned around and met them halfway.

"A dead guy," he explained. "A tramp, I think. Some tourists found him."

"Natural death?"

The constable shrugged his shoulders.

"I don't know," he said, unwilling to commit himself. "It looks like it. There's not a mark on him, if that's what you mean. No sign of violence. On the contrary, he looks real peaceful."

DeKok pressed through the circle of police officers and murmured a greeting. The dead man was leaning at an angle against the church wall. He was dressed in a stained, old green coat and high, worn boots, without socks. DeKok knelt down next to the corpse and looked at it carefully. There was a slight beard stubble around the chin and on the sunken cheeks. The half-open mouth with thick, purple lips was almost hidden under a bushy moustache. Well-formed, arched eyebrows and a network of fine wrinkles encircled the eyes. Grayish yellow hair peeked out from under a soft, felt hat.

The corpse did indeed look "peaceful". The legs crossed, the hands devoutly folded on the stomach, as if in prayer. It was a calm, serene sight, as if dying in the middle of a chilly May night, against a wet, mossy church wall was a mild happening, the thing to do.

DeKok rose slowly from his kneeling position and looked at Vledder.

"How old would you say?"

"Fifty-five, sixty," guessed the young Inspector. "Certainly not older. He's a bit neglected, looks unkempt. Maybe he's younger." He turned to one of the constables. "Did you find any papers?"

An older constable shook his head.

"I searched his pockets." He made an apologetic gesture. "As far as I could reach them without moving him."

"Found nothing?" asked Vledder who had a penchant for stating, or asking, the obvious.

"No, no wallet, no papers, no money. Nothing. Just a photo." The constable searched his own pockets. "A picture of a young woman," he added as he handed it over.

DeKok accepted the photograph and studied it. It was an old black and white photo. The edges were wrinkled and cracked and the upper right corner was missing altogether.

Vledder looked over DeKok's shoulder.

"A daughter?" he guessed.

"No, I don't think so." DeKok shook his head. This picture is between thirty and forty years old . . . at least. Look at the clothes, the hairdo. Probably from just before, or just after the war." The *war* to DeKok was World War II. "Early fifties at the latest." He turned the photo over and looked at the reverse. "Louise," he read out loud, "nineteen years."

"Nineteen and . . . let's say thirty five . . . that's fifty-four. She could be his wife."

DeKok nodded agreement.

"Unless the picture is older, or more recent. But it will do for now."

Bram Weelen, the police photographer, pushed himself roughly through the circle of constables. His heavy bag swung from one hand. He tapped DeKok on the shoulder.

"What do you need?"

DeKok waved vaguely around.

"Nothing special. Overviews from different angles and some close-ups. Also at least one full face and one profile. As clear as you can make them. I'll need to do the rounds with it."

"You don't know who he is?" Weelen placed his bag on the cobble stones.

"Not yet," admitted DeKok. "Perhaps I can find a clue from his clothes."

"Those rags?" grimaced Weelen. "Nothing but fleas, lice and a pair of pants stiff with urine."

"Well . . . I have to try something." DeKok shrugged his shoulders. "I mean, you know it's almost impossible to bury an unidentified corpse."

"How about burning it with the trash?" snorted Weelen.

DeKok turned suddenly toward the photographer. His eyes spat fire.

"Trash burning?" he hissed, "you should be burned with the trash . . . a foretaste of the hell you undoubtedly deserve."

The photographer paled. A bitter smile briefly curled his lips.

"All right, DeKok," he said weakly, "I'm sorry. It was just a joke."

"A bad . . . distasteful joke," observed DeKok, ice in his voice.

Weelen nodded to himself as he adjusted the focus for his first shots.

Dr. Koning, the Coroner, accompanied by two morgue attendants pulling a gurney, crossed the grass field. The old man, as usual, dressed in formal, striped pants, a swallow-tail coat and an old, greenish Garibaldi hat, was almost as colorful a personality as DeKok. DeKok greeted him heartily.

"Good morning, Doctor," he said cheerily. "For once I have a friendly corpse for you. Apparently no violence." He turned and pointed at the corpse. "See for yourself . . . how peaceful."

The eccentric Coroner looked at DeKok with an expressionless face.

"A dead person," he corrected sourly, "is neither friendly, nor peaceful. A dead person is a corpse and simply . . . dead."

He knelt down next to the dead man, placed his hand against the cold cheek and lifted the eyelids. He rose after just a few seconds. Deep wrinkles creased his forehead.

DeKok looked at him searchingly.

"A natural death?" asked the gray sleuth. His voice sounded hopeful.

The diminutive old doctor did not answer at once. He put both hands in his pockets and stared at one of the heavy buttresses of the church.

"It looks like an acute heart attack," he said softly, hesitatingly. "And maybe it is. There are also signs of suffocation."

"Suffocation?"

"Lack of breath," clarified Dr. Koning. "that's as far as I'll go and I advise you to keep it to yourself. I recommend an autopsy." He removed his old-fashioned pince-nez and started to clean the glasses. "I advise a thorough autopsy, including forensic. Dr. Rusteloos will probably be able to give you more details as soon as he's finished."

DeKok looked surprised.

"But why," he asked, a bit irritated, "why all that trouble? Surely there's nothing here that would indicate foul play?"

The doctor replaced his pince-nez and gave DeKok a penetrating look over the rim of his glasses.

"Have you ever," he began slowly, chidingly, "seen a man, or a woman, who peacefully folded their own hands as they died?"

DeKok was speechless.

"But surely that's not . . ."

"Impossible?" interrupted the old doctor. He sighed deeply and took one more look at the corpse. "No, it's not impossible." he went on, "but I've never seen it before."

DeKok, who inwardly kicked himself for having been so obtuse, swallowed his pride.

"You mean, I have to go to work, after all? It's not enough to establish his identity, but I also have to find his killer?"

The old doctor nodded slowly.

"I think you knew that already," he answered. "What we have here, DeKok, is a well-camouflaged murder." He placed a hand on DeKok's arm. "I know how you feel, old friend . . . sometimes I feel old and tired myself. But," he squeezed DeKok's arm encouragingly, ". . . there it is."

* * *

"Age . . . at least fifty-five; height . . . five feet nine; physical condition . . . reasonable; light gray eyes, unblemished lower teeth, caps on incisors in upper jaw, rather long, straw-blond, graying hair. No deformities, no scars, no tattoos, no birth marks."

"Fingerprints?"

"Kruger took them himself, also palm prints."

"Wounds?"

Vledder made a helpless gesture.

"No bruises, lacerations, contusions. Nothing, not a scratch. I don't know what got into Dr. Koning. As far as I could see, the body was completely whole."

"And the clothing?"

"Soiled . . . extremely dirty, especially the underwear. But it all *did* fit together well. Pants, jacket, shirt . . . it all seemed to be of first-class quality."

DeKok pursed his lips.

"No laundry marks, no manufacturing labels, no tailor's labels?"

Vledder shook his head.

"Forget about the clothes. Nothing to indicate anything there. All labels have been torn out."

DeKok looked up.

"Torn out! You don't say."

"I do say. But not recently . . . some time ago. The tears are not new, some places were definitely worn."

" . . . And no papers," sighed DeKok.

"Not even a scrap."

"What about the prints?"

"Kruger just called back."

"And?"

"He's not in our collection."

DeKok threw his pen on the desk.

12

"Here we go again," he said dejectedly. "Make up some story for the press. I've already seen the Commissaris* and he'll contact Dr. Rusteloos. Unless we hear to the contrary, the autopsy is tomorrow at ten." He raked his hands through his hair, as if trying to remember something. "What about Bram's pictures?"

Vledder tossed an envelope toward him. It landed with a soft thud exactly in front of DeKok.

"Just came in."

DeKok tore open the envelope and spread the photographs in front of him on the desk. Vledder left his own desk and stood next to him. There were twelve pictures . . . twelve times a man, resting easily in the pale sunlight of a beautiful day. Vledder shook his head.

"And that's supposed to be murder!" he exclaimed sarcastically.

DeKok nodded slowly, ignoring the tone of voice.

"Premeditated murder," he confirmed seriously.

Vledder went back to his desk and started to search through computer files. DeKok's computer terminal gathered dust on the corner of his desk. As far as anyone knew, he had never even turned it on. DeKok's loathing of all things modern was well known. He would have been perfectly happy living a hundred, two hundred years ago. He barely accepted the telephone and used cars as little as possible. His favorite mode of locomotion was on foot, to the despair of his colleagues, because he simply refused to carry a walkie-talkie. Even in the car he was known to shut off the communication gear. DeKok's early training was in a time when the police used phone booths and took cabs when necessary. He had a way of reminding people that in the 17th Century the Dutch

---

* Commissaris: a rank equivalent to Captain. There are only two ranks higher: Chief-Commissaris and Chief Constable. Each jurisdiction has only a single Chief Constable, the highest possible police rank. There is one Chief Constable for all of Amsterdam. Other ranks in the Municipal Police are: Constable, Constable First Class, Sergeant, Adjutant, Inspector, Chief-Inspector and Commissaris. Adjutants and below are equivalent to non-commissioned ranks. Inspector is a rank equivalent to 2nd Lieutenant.

maintained a world-wide empire without benefit of radio, television, telephone or telegraph. All communication was by sailing ship, horse back, stage coach or by means of one of the barges that would, pulled by a horse, criss-cross the Netherlands. There were times that DeKok positively ached for those by-gone days. It seemed to him that life was less of a rush, then, virtually free of stress . . . and people still managed to accomplish things, great things.

He reflected that he had spent more than thirty years in the Warmoes Street station, first as an uniformed constable and then, for the last twenty-five years or so, as a plain clothes policeman. The average tenure of an officer in Warmoes Street station, the busiest police station in Europe, was seldom more than five years. DeKok had put in more than thirty. He was old and tired, he reflected. Sometimes he longed for his well-deserved pension. What kept him going, he realized, was his love for the old city of Amsterdam and the always changing aspects of the Red Light District. Warmoes Station was situated at the edge of the Red Light District, the famous Quarter, where anything, legal, or illegal, could be had . . . for a price.

"Did you check missing persons?" asked DeKok.

"A whole bunch," grimaced Vledder. "These days there are far too many people who run away, desert, or disappear. The files are full of men who abandon their wives and women who abandon their husbands. It looks like an epidemic."

DeKok looked serious.

"Dissatisfaction," he said somberly, "with self, or with one's environment." He gestured, encompassing the world. "It's the main cause for disappearances these days."

"Well, they run in the hundreds," said Vledder, shrugging his shoulders. "And what does it get us? We don't even know the man's nationality. He could be an American tourist, a roaming Englishman, a French tramp. Toss it together and pick a number.

14

We're getting to be as cosmopolitan as Hell." He sighed elaborately. "It's about time we brand people."

"We're not cattle," said DeKok, sharp and disapproving.

Vledder had the grace to blush.

"But dammit," he argued feebly. "That eternal game of hide-and-seek causes a lot of work for us. It's always the same thing. You never know who you're hunting for. My name is Dick Vledder and I don't care who knows it." He pointed a finger in the air. "I have identification papers to prove it and I always carry them around. And I don't mind a brand, or whatever you want to call it. Why should I? I've nothing to hide."

"Not yet."

"What do you mean . . . not yet?" Vledder looked confused.

"Call it fate. You never know if you won't wind up in a situation where you'd prefer to remain anonymous."

"Nonsense . . . I would always . . ."

". . . be ready to accept the consequences of your actions?"

"Yes, I would." Vledder was positive.

"Well, it's moot anyway. There's no law that states that you have to be able to identify yourself. Holland . . . and I think the United States, is one of the few countries where that is so. In France, for instance, you may be arrested, simply for not carrying identification and you're required to produce it on demand. Here, as in the States, you're only required to identify yourself if you have committed a crime."

"Well, it's silly," spluttered Vledder, not clarifying exactly what was silly.

DeKok nodded calmly. He dropped the subject. He did not feel like having an argument with his young friend. Another sign of old age? He wondered about that. In his earlier days he would have reacted more strongly, but the years seemed to have mellowed him . . . even regarding those who divided the world in two groups . . . criminals and non-criminals. His world had become less black and white, good and bad, for and against. His world had become various shades of gray. Nothing was ever all one way, or another. Not when you dealt with people. He grinned to himself. His world had become as gray as his hair. He picked up Weelen's photographs and stuffed them back in the envelope.

The phone rang. Vledder picked it up and listened.

"There's a woman downstairs," he reported after a few seconds, "who wants to talk to you about the corpse. She read about it in the papers."

DeKok glanced at his watch. The evening papers had just about hit the streets.

"All right," he said, "have them send her up."

* * *

Vledder was waiting for her near the door of the large detective room. Her modest knock would certainly have been drowned out in the constant noise of the busy room. He opened the door for her and led her toward DeKok's desk at the far end. Another one, thought DeKok. He often had the feeling that he met more than his fair share of beautiful blondes, but as Vledder sometimes reminded him, beautiful blondes were almost an occupational hazard in Holland. There were certainly a lot of blondes and to DeKok all people were beautiful. He watched her as she approached.

Her gait had something ethereal about it, she seemed to float among the desks like a dancer who's feet barely touched the ground. The wavy, radiant blond hair billowed down to her shoulders and her figure elicited dreams of *houris* and eternal gardens of delight. More than one man glanced up as she passed and some of the female officers looked envious. She stopped in front of DeKok's desk and stretched out her hand to him.

"My name," she said in a soft, melodious voice, "is Abigail ... Abigail Manefeldt."

The gray sleuth had stood up and now he hesitated for just a moment, swallowed the bewitching influence she seemed to radiate and pressed her hand.

"DeKok," he said hoarsely, "DeKok with ... eh, with kay-oh-kay." Without taking his eyes off her he gestured in Vledder's direction. "Vledder, my colleague."

She looked from DeKok to Vledder and back again. Then she smiled politely.

"I read that in the paper," she said in friendly tone of voice. She reached for her heavy, leather shoulder bag, opened it and took a newspaper cutting from it. "About that unknown corpse ... the man who was found near South Church." She paused and looked at Dekok with a somber look. "I think I know who he is."

DeKok pointed at a chair next to his desk.

"Please sit down," he said. She sat down, crossed her legs and pulled her skirt over her knees. He waited until she was seated and then sank down in his own chair.

"It's but an idea," she said, "no more." She pushed the cutting toward DeKok. "The article is not very informative ... too little information to be definitive. That's why ... I would like to see the corpse." Her voice was calm, with an undertone of well-controlled emotion. "Is that possible?"

"You're missing someone?" asked DeKok, evading the question.

She loosened her expensive leather coat and nodded.

"My uncle."

DeKok looked at her intently, almost shamelessly. His observing glance travelled from her shoulders to her knees. He noted the expensive suit and estimated the price, he looked at her unblemished skin, the beautiful hands, the slender fingers with an excess of expensive jewelry and thought about the tramp they had found at the church wall.

"Your uncle?" There was incredulity in his voice.

"Archibald Manefeldt," she sighed, "my father's elder brother." She smiled wanly. "Very rich and very eccentric."

DeKok rubbed the bridge of his nose with a little finger.

"Eccentric enough to travel the world like a tramp?"

"Not exactly. But I wouldn't be at all surprised if it was him." She moved in her chair. "You see, Uncle Archibald wasn't really a tramp ... not a man who *needed* to live in the gutter. But sometimes he did ... for fun, make believe. It was his hobby."

"A strange hobby."

"Uncle Archibald liked people," she sighed. "He had a strongly developed sense of social responsibility. It was his goal to learn about people. Not just his own circle, you understand, but all layers of the population. In Paris he lived for a while as a *clochard*. He has lived in the most obscure places. For a while he was a doorman in a brothel, he washed dishes. He worked on the docks at one time." She smiled. "That was a complete disaster. He went through his knees the first time he tried to pick up a bale of something or other."

DeKok tapped the newspaper clipping with a forefinger.

"And why do you think that this may be your Uncle Archibald?"

She shrugged her shoulders.

"As I said ... it's just an idea. When I read the article I thought immediately of Uncle Archibald. The description is fairly accurate ... the age, the clothing."

"When did you see Uncle Archibald last?"

"About six months ago."

"Where?"

"At his home."

"And he's been missing ever since?"

"Since shortly thereafter ... yes."

"And you saw him regularly before his disappearance?"

"Yes, you might say that," she nodded. "Not that I saw him every day, or even every other day ... but I did see him regularly."

"Did you report him as missing?"

Abigail Manefeldt looked surprised.

"Me? No . . . perhaps his wife . . ."

"His wife?'

"Yes. She told me that Uncle Archibald had suddenly gone away . . . disappeared. I don't think she informed the police."

"Why not?"

"Uncle had those moods. He often took off. It wasn't something to be concerned about."

DeKok sighed.

"What's her address?"

"You mean Aunt?"

"Yes, Mrs. Manefeldt. Where does she live?"

A shadow fell across her face.

"Aunt . . . Aunt has passed away."

2

Vledder guided the aged VW handily through the old inner city, made a detour around the back of the Royal Palace, passed Town House Street and stopped with screeching brakes in front of the building that housed the police laboratories. They emerged from the car and crossed the wide sidewalk toward the flaked door. Vledder inserted a plastic card and the door opened. The penetrating smell of disinfectants and formaldehyde greeted them. They waved at the guard who had started to rise in his cubby-hole but who, upon seeing the familiar face of DeKok, sank back down to once again peruse his cross-word puzzle.

"You see," said Vledder as they proceeded down the corridors, "you can work for the police and have a nine-to-five job."

DeKok did not answer. It was not the first time that his partner had made this observation. Usually during a late night visit to the somewhat lugubrious old building. Until not too long ago Amsterdam had not even been able to boast a separate Homicide Division. It was small wonder that the authorities did not feel the need for a round-the-clock operation at the lab.

They reached the autopsy lab in the bowels of the building. DeKok found a light switch and bathed the chilling, tiled room in the merciless light of humming neon bars. Almost in the center, on a slanted, granite table was a body, covered with a sheet. Both Inspectors approached the table.

Abigail Manefeldt stopped in the door opening. Her slender fingers plucked nervously at a button of her expensive coat. Her nostrils quivered and small beads of perspiration clung to the almost invisible blonde down on her upper lip. DeKok motioned her closer.

Slowly, with dragging steps, she came closer. She stopped near the head end of the sinister table, her hands balled into fists, her teeth pressing down on her lower lip.

DeKok removed his hat, waited another second and then lifted a corner of the covering sheet. The face of the corpse became visible. In the bare, heartless light, without the background of the old, mossy church wall, the dead man presented a cold, revolting mask.

DeKok glanced at her.

"Is it . . .?"

Abigail shivered. She nodded slowly.

"Uncle Archibald," she whispered.

* * *

"Our Abigail was pretty upset," grinned Vledder. "For a moment there I thought she was going to faint. I was ready to catch her, but she remained upright." He made a comical gesture. "Anyway, at least we know who he is."

"Do we?" asked DeKok.

"But she identified him," said Vledder, astonished.

DeKok pushed his chair further back and placed his forearms on the desk. His friendly face, which often reminded one of a good-natured boxer, contorted into a grimace.

"Beautiful Abigail told us it was her Uncle Archibald."

Vledder seemed confused.

"Yes," he agreed slowly. "Just so. She was quite definite. Surely you heard her." There was a hint of sarcasm in his voice.

DeKok laughed.

"Oh, yes. I heard her all right. Without hesitation. Not even a nickel's worth of hesitation . . . if hesitation can be expressed in monetary values."

"So?" Vledder sounded irked. "What else do you want? She comes in response to a newspaper article, states she has lost her uncle, and recognizes the corpse. What's so strange about that?"

DeKok pushed his lower lip forward.

"Nothing," he said thoughtfully. "But for now she's the only one. I mean, we have no confirmation of the dead man's identity . . . whether or not he really is her uncle Archibald."

Vledder shook his shoulders.

"That's no problem," he said nonchalantly. "We have a starting point. There have to be other people who knew uncle Archibald when he was alive. We find one of them and if he, or she, also confirms that the corpse is that of Archibald Manefeldt, we're finished. Legally we're in the clear."

DeKok rubbed his face with a flat hand.

"And . . . if Dr. Rusteloos determines tomorrow that the man died of a simple heart attack, there's not a cloud left in our sky. We release the body to niece Abigail, she can take care of the funeral and . . ."

He was interrupted by a commotion in the corridor outside the detective room. The noise overcame the hubbub in the room itself. Soon the door slammed open and a small, unassuming little man stumbled into the room. Two uniformed constables towered over him. They kept a secure grip on the little man's shoulders and pushed him in the direction of DeKok's desk. DeKok lifted his legs from the desk and looked on in surprise as the group came closer. Meanwhile he wondered what sort of crime the little man could have committed. He knew him as Johan (Jan or Jack) Brewer.

"We just picked him up near the Central Railroad Station," announced one of the constables. "He was carrying a large packet of hashish, at least a pound . . . uncut . . . he was trying to sell it."

"We don't deal with hashish here." DeKok shook his head. "You better take him to Narcotics."

"We know that," said the constable calmly.

"Then . . . why bring him here?"

"He also had a wallet with money and papers."

"I have the same," smiled DeKok.

The constable growled something unintelligible. His face turned red.

"But the wallet was stolen, you see. There's no other way. You see . . . *his* name is Brewer, Johan Brewer. We also know him as Jack Stuff."

"I see, and who's wallet did he have?"

The constable consulted his notebook.

"Manefeldt . . . Archibald Manefeldt."

"Jan Brewer?"

"Yes, sir?"

DeKok looked at the little man, searched his memory.

"Didn't you used to sell condoms in the Quarter . . . some time ago?"

The little man lowered his head.

"Yes, in the old days . . . when it was still profitable. There was still some sort of morality in those days. Now, it's advertised in the papers, on television and displayed in shop windows. Times change. The girls buy them at the grocer's, or in the supermarket . . . by the gross, along with the milk and bread. It's become part of the service."

DeKok smiled.

"And now they call you Jack Stuff?"

The man grinned bitterly.

"From rubbers to stuff . . . what's the difference? The world is going to hell in hand-basket, anyway."

24

"What do you trade?"

"I don't trade." The little man shook his head. "I smoke it myself, though."

DeKok showed amazement.

"But the constables tell me . . ."

The little man sat down gingerly on the edge of a chair, a bitter smile on his pale face.

"I . . . eh," he confessed haltingly, "bought a piece, a block . . . from a Yank . . . nice stuff, real nice stuff. Almost pure. I tried some. I would have liked to keep it for myself. All of it. But, " he spread his arms, "a man has to make a living, right?"

"It must have cost you a bit," observed DeKok.

"What?"

"The hash . . . that piece . . . more than a pound?"

Jan Brewer shrugged his narrow shoulders.

"Reasonable . . . not bad."

"When did you buy it?"

"This afternoon . . . in town."

"You're independently wealthy now?"

Jack Stuff peered at DeKok.

"What do you mean?"

DeKok leaned forward.

"I mean," blustered DeKok, "that I know that you've been broke for months, you move from one place to another, sleep in the street sometimes. Yesterday morning you were begging for enough money to buy a cup of coffee, because you didn't want to ask your mother again." He paused, then continued in a calmer, friendlier tone of voice. "Come on, Jack, where did you get the money?"

The little crook moved restlessly in his chair.

"Found it . . ."

" . . . in an old sock, under the cobble stones," completed DeKok sarcastically. He shook his head disapprovingly. "Come on, Jack, no stories. Where did the money come from?"

A tic developed on the sunken cheeks of the petty criminal. His small hands twisted the sleeves of his jacket an his eyes darted around the room.

"As I said, as I told you . . . I found it."

DeKok leaned even closer, the last trace of friendliness had disappeared from his face, his eyes were cold and hard and his voice was like steel.

"Found it," he spat contemptuously. "Sure you found it . . . in the pockets of a sleeping man." He took a deep breath. "And when that poor man woke up while you were going through his pockets, you panicked and you killed him."

Jan Brewer stood up. His face was ashen, his cunning eyes were wide and frightened. He took a few paces backward, shaking his head, raising his hands in a defensive gesture.

"No," he uttered shrilly. "No," he repeated louder.

DeKok was not impressed. He came around the desk and placed himself in front of the little man, big, angry, threatening.

"You killed him," he accused. "Yes, Jack, you killed him for . . . money." The contempt in DeKok's voice could be cut with a knife.

"It isn't true."

"Yes, it is. You had already figured, right from the start, how much hash you could buy for the money. Your little diseased mind planned it all." He tapped the forehead of Jack Stuff. "Right here, in that petty little brain of yours, the brain you've been ruining with all sort of poisons for as long as I've known you." DeKok's eyes narrowed to mere slits. "When that old man felt your hands on his body, he woke up and you had to do something." He brought his face to within inches of that of the frightened crook. "Tell me, Jack, what did you do?"

Brewer shook his head in despair. In his fear for the big man, he walked backward until he stumbled over a chair and fell on his back. DeKok leaned forward, gripped him by the front of his shirt and lifted him to his feet with one mighty heave.

"You had no choice, Jack," he said with unctuous sarcasm. "After all, it wasn't really your fault, was it? It was that guy's own fault. He should have stayed asleep, should never have wakened. He shouldn't have done it."

The little man swallowed with difficulty. His adam's apple bobbed nervously up and down.

"He never woke up," he screamed. "It isn't true. He never woke up. He *couldn't* wake up." Brewer raised his hands as if summoning the heavens to witness. "That guy was as dead as a doornail. And what good is money to a stiff? Everything is free in Heaven."

* * *

"What are we going to do with that guy?"

DeKok sighed deeply and lifted the telephone with a reluctant motion.

"I'll inform the Commissaris. You call Narcotics. Tell him we'll deliver the hash to the lab, but that we'll keep Brewer for the time being."

"On what charge?"

"Theft," suggested DeKok vaguely. "As long as we don't know how Archibald died, we can hardly charge him with murder."

"Well, you almost had him convicted," grinned Vledder. "I thought you'd lost it. The poor guy seemed close to a heart attack."

"I know Jan Brewer," smiled DeKok. "It isn't the first time that I tangled with him. I know exactly how he is. You get nowhere with sweet words." He scratched the back of his neck. "Anyway," he admitted candidly, "I had to try *something*. Who could predict that before the autopsy, somebody would show up with the victim's papers."

"You really think he's got something to do with Manefeldt's death?"

DeKok replaced the receiver without making the call.

"That's hard to say," he said pensively. "His explanation was quite reasonable. I mean, an old acquaintance treats him to a few beers and afterward our Jack staggers, slightly drunk, through the streets. No money, no place to live. He's looking for a place to sleep for a while. Then he sees a man peacefully slumped against the church wall, nicely sheltered from the wind by one of the buttresses. He stretches out next to the man and starts a friendly conversation. Then he suddenly realizes the man is dead. The shock sobers him up. He crawls away and starts running. About two streets later he thinks better of it, goes back and searches the corpse."

"It *could* have been that way."

DeKok grinned to himself.

"I loved his justification." He raised his hands in the air and imitated Brewer's stance and tone of voice. "*And what good is money to a stiff? Everything is free in Heaven.*"

"And what about Hell?" Vledder wanted to know.

DeKok ignored the question.

"Still," he mused, "that remark about Heaven touched me."

"How's that?"

"The thought behind it," reflected DeKok. "The association. Jan Brewer found a corpse at the church wall, a peaceful corpse . . . a man who had, apparently, died calmly and for who, so it seemed, the Gates of Heaven were opened wide."

"I see what you mean," said Vledder. "Jack Stuff took the wallet but didn't change anything else. Therefore he probably found Manefeldt in the same position as we did."

"With piously folded hands," nodded DeKok.

* * *

They left the station together, DeKok leading the way, dressed in a comfortable old jacket and his ever present, decrepit little felt hat

28

far back on his head. Young Vledder followed close behind, the epitome of the young, eager policeman, in a neat gray suit, the blond hair immaculately groomed.

DeKok had invited his young partner for a few drinks in the bar of Little Lowee. They had earned it, judged DeKok. The day had started early and had been enervating. But that was not the only reason. Little Lowee poured the best cognac in town.

They strolled leisurely through the Quarter, observed the hordes of visitors, noted that the sex-theaters, some with live shows, were busy and that most of the whores had the curtains closed, indicating that they were "occupied". Most of the denizens of the Red Light District knew and respected DeKok. They greeted him politely, cheerfully, or formally, depending on their perceived status in the mind of the gray sleuth. DeKok nodded to one and all as he passed by. Vledder was ignored by most, except that some of the prostitutes cast appreciative glances at the tall, handsome young man.

They paused in front of the establishment of German Lou. There was a quarrel. Screeching female voices and angry male voices emerged from the brothel. A drunk sailor was forcibly ejected and landed with a smack on the pavement. German Lou, a woman bigger and possibly stronger than DeKok, appeared in the door opening, dusting her hands. She cursed the befuddled man, accused him of ignorance and impotence. The passers-by laughed. The sailor scrambled to his feet and rearranged his clothing. Then he staggered away.

The two cops followed the sailor for a while, just to be sure. When they saw him enter a bar, they turned off and soon they sidled into the intimate little bar of Little Lowee.

* * *

Little Lowee lived up to his name. He was a small, skinny man with a friendly, mousy face and a heart that was as large as it was crooked. He smiled happily when he discovered DeKok. Lowee considered DeKok a particular friend and DeKok always had a soft spot for the small barkeeper. The fact that DeKok represented the Law was ignored by Lowee. Friends were entitled to their foibles.

"Been a long time," chirped Lowee.

DeKok hoisted himself on a stool at the end of the bar, his back to the wall. From there he had a good view of the room. Vledder took the stool next to him. It was quiet in the bar, as was to be expected. Most of the tables were empty. The bar was primarily a gathering place for off-duty prostitutes and Vledder and DeKok had seen with their own eyes how good business was for the members of the world's oldest profession.

Lowee wiped his hands on his shirt.

"Same recipe?"

He dived underneath the counter and produced a special bottle of cognac, kept there for DeKok's exclusive use. Almost in the same motion he placed three large snifters in a row. DeKok looked on with an indulgent smile on his face. He was a connoisseur of cognac and loved the little ritual with the bottle and the glasses. With a steady hand Lowee poured his usual, generous measures.

"Busy?" he asked conversationally.

DeKok lifted his glass with a reverent movement and took a sip. He savored the taste and the aroma for a long moment. Then he nodded slowly and absent-mindedly produced the envelope with Weelen's photographs from an inside pocket. Carefully he spread them on the bar and took another sip from his drink.

"You know him?"

Lowee looked surprised. In the District he knew almost as many people as DeKok, although their acquaintances did not always coincide.

"Of course I does . . . the Baron."

"The Baron?" grinned Vledder.

Lowee righteously ignored the brash young man and addressed himself exclusively to DeKok. After all, Vledder was a *cop*, but DeKok was a friend.

"Tha's what we calls him . . . the Baron," continued Lowee, as if Vledder had not spoken. "He roams around here. Squats somewheres inna old building. Near New Market I thinks. Comes for a beer every now and then."

"Often?'

Lowee shrugged his shoulders.

"Like I says, sometimes . . . onna beets."* He cocked his head. "Whadda you want, live and let live, I says, I just forgets about it."

"How do you mean?"

Lowee grimaced.

"Ain't never gonna pay me. Ain't got no money. Lives on begging."

DeKok nodded his understanding.

"Why do they call him the Baron?"

"He'll tells you alla time he's been rich. Poor nobelelity. Lost their loot. So . . . Baron." The barkeeper placed a hand over his heart. "But iffen it's true . . .?" He grinned, waved a rag around as if it were a scepter. "Them guys have them fantastic tales. You cain't believe 'em." He sighed. "To tell you the truth, DeKok, I thinks he's one of them actors, down on their luck."

"Why do you say that?"

"Hey, DeKok, you gives 'em two beers and he'll starts with them Shakespeare stuff." He bowed his head, looked intently at the rag in his hand. "To be or not to be," he declaimed in a sepulchral voice.

DeKok laughed heartily.

"A great talent has been lost with you."

Onna beets, Amsterdam bastardization (underworld slang) for "on the beach", meaning broke, or living on credit.

31

The small barkeeper grinned broadly.

"Whether it's better to suffer the slings and arrows of outrageous cops," he joked, losing his gutter language momentarily. "I got it, you knows, man, I gotta talent for them things."

DeKok replaced the photos's in the envelope.

"I appreciate your other talents more," he said. "Pour again, please."

Lowee grabbed the bottle, tilted it and then hesitated. The cheerful look on his face disappeared.

"Whadda you wants with the Baron?" he asked suspiciously. "Something the matter with him, is it? Why them pictures?"

DeKok did not answer at once.

"The undiscovered country, from whose bourn no traveller returns," quoted DeKok.

Lowee looked at him searchingly and then proved that he was indeed familiar with Hamlet's soliloquy.

"He's dead," he concluded.

DeKok merely nodded. Lowee's hands shook as he refilled the glasses.

3

Dr. Rusteloos, the police pathologist, was in a hurry. He had another three autopsies scheduled for that day. He did not speak, but merely gave DeKok a friendly nod as he came in and started to work. His sharp lancet slid downward from the neck, across the breast to the tight belly. Then he made two additional cuts, from near each shoulder to just below the neck. He pushed the skin out of the way and removed the breast bone. Then he pushed the ribs aside, all the while softly murmuring in the microphone around his neck. The microphone was connected to a small tape-recorder in his pocket and allowed him to review his notes at a later date.

Within minutes the pathologist had opened Archibald Manefeldt's body and started his examination of the organs. DeKok looked on with interest. In most cases he would leave the attendance at the autopsy to Vledder. But this case intrigued him. Almost right from the start when Dr. Koning had pointed out the dichotomy of a dead man with devoutly folded hands. In his heart he knew the old Coroner was right, but he hoped against hope, that Manefeldt had died a peaceful, natural death. That is why he was here. He hoped that Dr. Rusteloos would be able to confirm his belief. The sooner he knew the better.

As he watched the pathologist, his chances of a "natural death" verdict seemed to become slimmer with each passing moment. Dr. Koning was no fool, he had seen thousands of

33

corpses. If he thought there was something suspicious about this one, DeKok would, albeit reluctantly, have to agree. He took a step back. The sweet, sick-making smell of the opened body made him feel queasy. It did not seem to bother Dr. Rusteloos, who worked steadily on.

Suddenly the rhythm was interrupted. The expression on the physician's face changed. A look of astonishment appeared in the blue eyes above the mask. He leaned forward and placed the knife back on the instrument table. With a hand-held shower head, he rinsed off the heart. Now DeKok could see it as well. He came closer, forgot all about the smell. In the lower left chamber of the heart was a thin, hollow pin, barely a millimeter thick.

* * *

Vledder looked with incredulity at his old partner.

"What!?" he exclaimed with a shocked voice.

"A hypodermic needle," answered DeKok tonelessly.

"In the heart?"

"Left lower chamber. Broken off. More than likely because of a strong contraction . . . cramp."

Vledder shook his head in astonishment.

"I don't understand it. How is it possible? I looked him over very carefully. There wasn't a mark on him. The morgue attendants didn't see anything, either. There was no blood on the shirt."

DeKok scratched the back of his neck.

"That . . . wasn't necessary," he said slowly. "If the killer was an expert . . ."

"Was he?"

"Dr. Rusteloos didn't want to say anything about that." He shrugged his shoulders. "He didn't commit himself . . . talked about an intracardial injection, initiated to the left of the breast

34

bone, between the fourth and fifth rib. That's what he wrote in his report and that's about it."

"That spot . . . between the fourth and fifth rib . . . is that the right spot?"

"Yes, that's the place to administer an injection to the heart."

"Aha . . . an expert."

"That's difficult to establish." DeKok sounded dejected. "Also . . . the broken off needle indicates an inexperienced hand." He paused, rubbed his chin. "We'd be wrong," he continued, "to immediately look in the direction of a medically educated man, or woman . . . There are many possibilities. Just think of the number of addicts that are able to handle a needle and there are others who handle needles on a daily basis, diabetics, for instance. The hypodermic is no longer restricted to the medical profession."

"Did he die because of the broken needle?"

"That was not the immediate cause of death."

"What was?"

"Opium."

"Opium?" Vledder was confronted with another surprise.

"Strongly concentrated opium," confirmed DeKok.

"You mean the stuff that the Chinese smoke in pipes?"

"Exactly. Brown smoking opium, dissolved in water and injected directly into the heart."

Both remained silent. Their thoughts returned to the previous morning . . . the pale sunlight, the peaceful corpse at the wall of the South Church. Vledder finally broke the silence.

"Dr. Koning was right . . . it *was* murder."

DeKok raked his fingers through his hair.

"The old fox," he said, shaking his head, "I tried to talk him out of it, but he was right. I didn't really believe it until now. I'll have to beg his pardon, next time I see him."

"You should, he'll be flattered." Vledder stared into the distance. "How did he spot it?" he wondered. "It couldn't have just been the hands."

"What?" asked DeKok absent-mindedly.

"That it wasn't a natural death ... How did Dr. Koning know?"

"Maybe he looked at the pupils. They were enlarged because of the opium. I didn't pay much attention to it at the time. I knew Koning was right behind us and, frankly, the total picture, the peaceful scene, lulled me into forgetting all about a possible crime. I muffed it."

Vledder grinned.

"I'm sure the perpetrator was counting on that."

DeKok's face suddenly hardened.

"The perpetrator," he repeated glumly. "You're right. A murder means a murderer. Somebody who, for one reason or another, robs a fellow human being of life." He seemed to snap out of his disheartened mood. "That'll be our task from now on," he added in a determined voice, "enough dilly-dallying, wishes won't come true anyway."

He went over to the coat rack and retrieved his ridiculous little hat.

"Come on," he said grimly, "we're going to pay a visit to Count's Gate."

"That's where the beautiful Abigail resides," knew Vledder.

* * *

They walked across Chalk Market, took the bridge across Regent's Canal and turned right toward Count's Gate. They stopped in front of number 37 and looked up at the pretty 17th Century neck-gable that appeared recently to have been restored to its original luster. A bright green door at the far side of a bluestone stoop was decorated with a brass knocker in the shape of a lion's head. The white curly letters on the high-gloss door announced: *Abigail Manefeldt, Beauty Consultant.*

"Beauty Consultant," said DeKok, half to himself, as if planting it firmly in his memory.

Vledder looked at his partner. Observed the craggy face with the expression of a good-natured boxer, the wide, slightly flattened nose, the wild, bushy eyebrows and the unruly, gray hair that peeked from under his little hat. He grinned.

"Well," he remarked laconically, "we're at the right address. It's about time they try to fix you up a little."

DeKok lifted the heavy door-knocker and let it drop against the brass strike plate.

"All right," he said agreeably, "I'll ask if they can do something about my exterior." He pulled in his stomach and pushed his chest out. "It should be a challenge."

Vledder pursed his lips, and shook his head sadly.

"More than a challenge, I'm afraid, I see it more as a *Mission Impossible*."

DeKok smiled thinly as the green door opened slowly.

A wide-shouldered young man appeared in the door opening. DeKok estimated him to be less than thirty years old. He had an olive colored skin, thick, black, wavy hair, a crooked nose and large dreamy eyes underneath dark eyebrows. A faint smile played around the weak mouth. He leaned forward and looked questioningly at the two men.

DeKok lifted his hat.

"My name is DeKok, DeKok with kay-oh-kay." He pointed a thumb at Vledder. "This is my colleague, Vledder. We're police inspectors."

"Inspectors?" The surprise in the man's voice seemed genuine.

"Yes," nodded DeKok. "We wanted to have another chat about the sad passing of Uncle Archibald." He paused, gave a winning smile. "You knew Uncle Archibald?"

"No," the man shook his head, "Much to my regret. He must have been an interesting man . . . or so I've heard."

37

"Eccentric . . . out of the ordinary?"

"Yes, according to the stories . . ." He did not complete the sentence, but stepped aside. "But don't just stand there outside. Please, come in. Abigail will be glad to receive you."

They entered the marble corridor. The house was laid out as so many Amsterdam houses are. A long corridor running from front to back, rooms on either side and a staircase halfway down the corridor, leading to other floors. Amsterdam houses tended to be long and narrow. Because real estate taxes used to be based on the amount of footage that actually faced the street, the early Dutch had found something to negate the impact of the taxes. Some houses were narrow and some were pie-shaped, exposing a minimum amount of facade to the street. There is a house in Amsterdam that is exactly as wide as its narrow front-door. When it comes to saving money, the Dutch have been known to go to extremes.

Meanwhile the man preceded them, politely, subservient like a butler. DeKok wondered how much of the man's attitude was fake, how much was just a pose.

The room was spacious and high with heavy rafters supporting the ceiling. The walls were stark, bare and white. A diffused light from a strip of small windows illuminated somber, heavy oak furniture.

Abigail Manefeldt met them, bewitching, with outstretched hand and a bright smile on her face. She was dressed in a long, purple dress of rough tweed with a low, scooped out decollete and short sleeves. The borders were decorated with a black strip in a Greek pattern.

DeKok shook hands. Meanwhile he studied her. She *was* beautiful, he observed again . . . fascinating. He held her gaze for several seconds, then he released her hand. His gaze went from the startling blue eyes to the half-open mouth and from the slender neck toward the sweet swelling of the breasts. The purple dress intrigued him. He had the feeling that she wore nothing underneath, that the coarse material rested directly on her naked skin. It was an exciting thought that he covered hastily with a shy laugh.

Abigail waved vaguely.

"You've already met my husband?"

"I didn't know you were married," said DeKok.

She laughed coquettishly.

"Perhaps I should have said my *future* husband," she corrected.

"Oh."

She cocked her head at him, a twinkling in her eyes.

"Surely the police aren't *that* puritanical, not in Amsterdam."

"Not the police." DeKok shook his head. "But the law . . . *future* husbands are not mentioned. It's not a legal concept."

She took the man by an arm and pressed her body against him.

"But we're going to get married, aren't we, Raymond?"

"If only to soothe the conscience of the Inspector." The man laughed politely at his own joke.

DeKok could not let it pass.

"An inelegant, almost insulting reason for marriage," he countered. He took another good look at the man. "Raymond . . .?"

The man disentangled himself from a clinging Abigail and bowed formally.

"Raymond . . . Raymond Verbruggen."

DeKok gave him an amiable smile.

"The decision to get married is a recent one?"

"We've known each other for about a year," said Abigail nonchalantly, but it sounded like an apology.

"That's . . . a long time."

"Sure."

"And has he already been introduced to the family?"

"Of course," she seemed puzzled. "Raymond has already been completely accepted."

"I see . . . also by Uncle Archibald?"

Abigail glanced aside. She seemed taken aback.

"Raymond has never had the opportunity to meet Uncle Archibald." Her voice was unsure, hesitating. "He was never there."

"Who?"

"Uncle Archibald. He was always away. Aunt Helen was used to that, she didn't know any better. Came Spring, Uncle Archibald would disappear. When the leaves started to drop from the trees, he would return."

"A strange man."

"Yes, he was." She nodded to herself. "I told you at the station . . . rich and eccentric."

DeKok rubbed the bridge of his nose with a little finger.

"If you have a lot of money, you can afford to be eccentric."

Abigail did not react. DeKok looked at his little finger as if he had never seen it before. Finally he put his hand down.

"Are there children?"

She shook her head.

"Uncle Archibald never wanted children. He used to say . . . a couple doesn't *have* children, children *own* the parents."

"And he didn't want to be owned," grinned DeKok.

"I think so," she said distantly.

"Are you the sole heir?"

"I don't know exactly." She looked bored and sighed. "There is, I think, a cousin on Aunt's side."

DeKok chewed his lower lip, deep in thought.

"What did Aunt Helen die of?" he asked after a long pause.

"I think her heart." She shrugged and for a heart-stopping moment it looked as if her breasts would bob up out of her dress. All three men seemed to hold their breath. DeKok swallowed his confusion.

"Did she have a history of heart trouble?" he persisted.

"That . . . that I don't know."

DeKok stared at her, tried his best smile.

"You must have visited your aunt often, during the long summer months."

"Especially as a child. I used to spend my vacations there."

"And later?"

"I visited her often."

"Then . . . surely you would know if she had a weak heart."

Abigail paused. Her tongue darted out and licked her dry lips. She was visibly nervous, confused. She rocked from one leg onto the other and her fingers plucked at the belt of her dress.

"I never noticed," she said softly.

"Did she die unexpectedly?"

"Yes, rather suddenly."

"You were surprised?"

Raymond Verbruggen interrupted. He was agitated and showed it.

"What are you leading up to?" he asked sharply. "Can't you see you're upsetting her." He took a threatening step closer. "Is this an official interrogation?"

"You could call it that," admitted DeKok blandly. "You see, I'm wondering if Aunt Helen really died a natural death."

Raymond Verbruggen stared at him. The dreamy look had left his eyes. His gaze was hard, alert and suspicious.

"Really? Meaning . . . what?"

"You might well ask. Uncle Archibald, you see, died of an intracardial injection with opium. It was murder."

Abigail screamed. It was a strange, raw, scream. She closed her eyes and her head fell to one side. Vledder rushed forward, managed to catch her and eased her to the floor.

4

They walked back the way they had come. A friendly sun caressed the Montelbaan Tower, a frequent subject of painters and photographers. It is considered to be Amsterdam's most perfectly proportioned tower, just a stone's throw away from the Rembrandt House. The same sun mirrored playfully in the murky green of the canals and nurtured some young people of the leather-jacket variety, lazily sunning themselves in old garden furniture on top of a dilapidated houseboat. DeKok scratched the back of his neck and wondered if these particular people had known Archibald. Possibly . . . possibly not.

All over the city, thousand of families lived on houseboats. This part of town was full of old houseboats and empty warehouses. Most were used as crash-pads by a generation that could not forget the early sixties and seventies. DeKok smiled at the thought. In those days a number of "hippies" had actually been elected to the City Council. A lot of former "hippies" still remained, a bit longer in the tooth, but still striving after the Bohemian lifestyle that would never return. The flower children from yesterday had been replaced with daydreamers, opium smokers, hash growers and other drug addicts.

Yet, the area had been able to retain the somewhat moderate, broad-minded attitude of Amsterdam. In this part of Amsterdam, as in the neighborhood of the Red Light District, respected business men lived next door to brothels, or drug dealers. A church could be found next door to a bar. And everything was leavened with the tolerant "live and let live" attitude of the true Amsterdammer.

Here too, noticed DeKok, the wonderful mixture of Amsterdam was epitomized by the dilapidated houseboat and its neighbor. Right next to the wreck was moored a neat, trim version of the same houseboat. Brightly painted and immaculately clean. The residents had lifted about a dozen cobblestones on either side of their gang plank and had planted a row of geraniums in the earth. Sooner or later, DeKok knew, somebody from Municipal Works would notice the desecration of the quay pavement and then, in the fullness of time, a few Municipal workers would come to uproot the flowers and replace the cobblestones. About a week later, the houseboat owner would lift the stones again and plant new flowers . . . maybe tulips, hoped DeKok.

The gray sleuth reluctantly forced his eyes away from a painter on the sidewalk and glanced at Vledder who silently walked next to him. Apparently the young Inspector was still under the spell of the beautiful Abigail, who, for a few seconds, he had been able to hold in his strong arms. DeKok guessed the trend of his thoughts.

"You were just in time," he said.

"I saw it coming," smiled Vledder. There was a tenderness in his voice that made DeKok look closer. "I already noticed it in the lab," continued Vledder, "Abigail Manefeldt has weak nerves. She can't handle that sort of thing. She's too fragile, too sensitive."

"She fainted," grimaced DeKok.

"Were you surprised?"

"What *do* you mean? Why shouldn't I be surprised?"

Vledder gesticulated wildly.

"You're firing one question after another at her. You ask about the death of her aunt, you ask her if she will gain by the death of her uncle and when she gets upset, you tell her, straight out, that her uncle has been murdered." The young Inspector grinned without mirth. "I ask you . . . how much can you expect from a woman, from anybody, under those circumstances."

"I don't like women who faint," said DeKok, shrugging his shoulders.

"Why not?"

"It's too difficult to determine if it's for real, or just comedy."

"This was no comedy," said Vledder sharply. "Didn't I hold her in my arms? It was a direct result of your heartless attack." It sounded reproachful. "You've *got* something against her. Did . . . right from the start. You don't trust her because . . . because . . ."

". . . she has a motive," said DeKok frostily.

He halted in mid-stride, pushed his hat a little farther back on his head and looked at his young partner.

"Listen my boy," he said patiently, "there are a number of strange circumstances surrounding the death of uncle Archibald. The more I think about, the more I'm convinced that the man, or woman, who killed him, was extremely cunning. Take for instance . . . the presentation."

"Presentation?"

"Yes, the way in which the corpse was presented, the way we found it . . . friendly, peaceful and outwardly undamaged, leaning against an old church wall. If Dr. Koning had not insisted, I might have ignored the discrepancies altogether. I told you I never looked at the eyes, for instance. Anyway . . . if it hadn't been for that, Manefeldt's death would have been a mystery . . . written off as a natural death." He paused, took a deep breath. "And then there's the money."

"What money?"

"The money the dead man carried around," sighed DeKok. "In the wallet that Jack Stuff took off him, there was enough money to buy twice the amount of hashish he bought. He bought more than a pound. He could have bought more than a kilo. Let's face it, according to the current rate of exchange, we're talking about several thousands. Well, that's what Jack lifted. But, according to Lowee, Manefeldt lived 'onna beets', and wasn't even able to pay for his beer."

"That means nothing," argued Vledder. "It was his temporary life style. Manefeldt was rich. If he had really needed money, he could have just gone to the bank."

"Exactly." DeKok narrowed his eyes to mere slits. "That's exactly it," he said bleakly. "He could have just gone to the bank. I thought the same thing. But I checked with a bank connection and it's pretty clear that Manefeldt hasn't withdrawn a nickel from his account, not since last October thirteen."

They walked on, DeKok with his typical, somewhat waddling gait, Vledder pensive, a crease in his forehead. He was not wondering about DeKok's ability to obtain information about a bank account. He took that in stride. The average cop would need a warrant or, at the very least, the ability to show probable cause. But DeKok could just pick up the phone and have that sort of information in almost no time at all. The most remarkable thing about it was, reflected Vledder, that DeKok did not think it remarkable at all.

"He could have kept the money," Vledder opined, "In case of emergencies."

"You mean, he's been carrying that amount of cash since last October?"

"Why not?"

DeKok did not answer. It was one of his infuriating habits that he was able to ignore things with a sublime indifference when it suited him. It was as if he had not heard a thing. At the end of the Regent's Canal, they took a short-cut along Crooked Tree Ditch and soon they arrived at the South Church. The beautiful Hemony Carillon in the belfry was silent. The growl of the traffic about a hundred yards away, seemed muted.

DeKok stopped and looked at the place where they had found the corpse against the mossy wall, sheltered between two wide, massive buttresses. Vledder squatted down next to one of the buttresses. His face was serious.

"You think he was killed right here?"

"No," answered DeKok, thoughtfully rubbing the bridge of his nose with a little finger, "no, I don't think so. I think the actual murder was committed elsewhere and that the corpse was placed here on purpose. There are some indications."

"Such as?"

"You noticed some of it yourself. Remember, you said there was no blood on the shirt." He grimaced. "That wasn't allowed, you see. It didn't fit in with the killer's plans."

"What plans?"

"The intent was that we should be misled. It wasn't supposed to look like murder. If we had discovered only the tiniest spot of blood on the inside of the shirt, we would have started to look for the cause and we would almost certainly have discovered the puncture mark."

Vledder rose to his feet.

"That could mean that Archibald wasn't wearing a shirt at the time of the injection."

"I've inquired," nodded DeKok. "It isn't easy to give an intracardial injection. You have to feel for the right ribs in order to find the correct spot. The posture in which we found the corpse . . . sitting . . . would have made it unnecessarily difficult. That's why I'm almost convinced that the victim, at the time of the injection, was in a supine position, with bared chest."

"Voluntarily?" panted Vledder.

"Perhaps." DeKok spread his arms in a helpless gesture. "Who can say? Maybe he was tricked by some sort of proposal. Perhaps the perpetrator was clumsy, nervous. Perhaps Manefeldt realized at the last moment what was about to happen and struggled, struggled so hard that the needle broke." He sighed again. "Who can say?"

"The murderer!"

It was a new voice.

The two Inspectors turned as one. They beheld a strangely dressed man. DeKok estimated him to be in late thirties, early forties. He wore tight jeans with patches and a black shirt underneath a grimy, fur jacket. A ban-the-bomb emblem dangled from a chain around his neck. He rocked slightly on his feet and smiled shyly.

"Sorry, I overheard part of your conversation. I couldn't help it." He nodded in DeKok's direction. "I bet you're Inspector DeKok, isn't that so? I heard about you. Aren't you in charge of the Baron's murder?"

DeKok looked at him searchingly, His sharp gaze traveled from the shaking hands to the sallow face.

"Murder?" he asked.

The man smiled again.

"It *was* murder, wasn't it?"

"Apparently," answered DeKok in a friendly voice, "you know more than I do. Mr. . . . eh, the Baron is dead. That's all we're sure of."

The man stopped smiling.

"It was murder," he said evenly.

"You have proof, evidence?"

"Of course I've got evidence." The man nodded vehemently. "I saw it coming. I warned him, I told him it would happen."

DeKok's eyebrows suddenly rippled in a way that did not seem possible. They seemed completely detached from his forehead and undulated in a manner that was both mesmerizing and incomprehensible. Many people thought that DeKok's eyebrows lived a life of their own. And at times they did seem to do just that. At times they seemed to resemble two hairy caterpillars dancing a wild dance to an unheard, primeval rhythm. The man seemed hypnotized by the sight. He came out of his daze as the movement on DeKok's forehead subsided and the old sleuth repeated his question.

"You warned him about murder?"

"Yes," answered the man, shaking his head as if to clear his vision. He obviously did not believe what he had just seen. "He asked for it."

"Asked for it?" DeKok tone was one of disbelief.

"In a manner of speaking." The man gestured vaguely. "He seemed to attract danger . . . if you know what I mean. He seemed to defy it, daring it to do its worst."

DeKok nodded his understanding.

"You knew him well?"

A transported look came in the man's eyes.

"I was his friend. We lived together . . . more than three months. Big Pierre and the Baron . . . that's what it says on our shingle. A real shingle on a real front door, a door with a heavy padlock." He pointed at the church. "Right behind here, in Sand Cross Street."

"An abandoned building?"

"Yes, we're squatters. It's been declared uninhabitable, but it's solid. We have everything . . . a tight roof, windows, water, electricity."

"And you're Big Pierre?"

"That's what they call me. I'm from the north, but I lived in Paris for a few years. I'm from Friesland originally." He made a deprecating movement with his hand. "You know, the province of cattle and dairy products, where it's easier to trace the lineage of a cow, than of a person. I'm from a small town near the sea. Less than a thousand people, but more than a hundred thousand cows . . . all prime, registered Frisians . . . the cows, I mean, not the people. My real name is Eduard Jelle Douwinga." He sighed "But you can forget that as soon as you've heard it. Now I'm Big Pierre. I like it."

DeKok smiled.

"Do you know the Baron's real name?"

"Sure, Manefeldt, with an aristocratic 'dt' at the end."

"Did he tell you?"

"No."

"Then how do you know?"

Big Pierre lowered his head.

"I went through his papers."

"When?"

"A few days ago, while he was asleep."

"Why?"

"As I said . . ." He swallowed. "I was afraid something was going to happen to him. Somebody should be able to alert his family . . . right?"

DeKok stared at him for several long seconds.

"How much money did the Baron carry?"

Pierre avoided his eyes.

"I didn't pay any attention to that."

DeKok smiled sarcastically.

"How much?" he asked in a compelling voice.

The man shook his head.

"It wasn't about money," he exclaimed, irritated. "Not at all. Why should it? The Baron was a good man. We shared everything. It wasn't to steal. I just wanted his name and address."

"You could have asked," snorted DeKok.

"I did," admitted the man, "but he didn't want to tell me."

"Why not . . . I thought you were friends?"

The man made a helpless gesture.

"In many ways the Baron was a strange man. He never wanted to talk about the past. *The past is dead*, he used to say."

A long silence followed, finally broken by Vledder.

"And . . . have you done it?"

"Done what?"

"Informed his family."

A sad look came into the man's eyes.

"I was there."

"Where?"

"His house in Seadike . . . near Sheep's Drift. The Baron was rich, did you know that? A nice house . . . a small castle . . . a large garden. But there was nobody there. Everything was locked up. I looked around. The garden had been neglected and weeds grew between the tiles of the terrace." He paused. "At first I didn't want to get involved. After all, it's not without risk. I should have left it to the family to find out on their own. But I'm afraid the Baron has no family left." He looked at DeKok. "That's why I looked you up."

"To tell me it was murder?"

Pierre stared at one of the buttresses and did not answer at once.

"They caught him," he said finally.

"Who?"

"The dealers," he said after some hesitation.

* * *

"Dealers . . . drug dealers . . . and a murderer who uses opium." There was mockery in DeKok's voice. "Excellent, really excellent . . . completely in style."

Vledder looked perplexed.

"I found Big Pierre's story quite plausible," he protested indignantly. "No reason to be so sarcastic. Just think, Archibald Manefeldt, alias the Baron, not an addict himself, during one of his 'walk-abouts', winds up in the dreary world of the addicts. He observed how the pitiful victims are exploited by the brute dealers. The Baron, as we know, was a man with a social conscience and he decided to do something about it. He poses as an addict, learns the identity of the dealers and commits treason. Every time they make an appointment, he supplies the Narcotics Division with time and place."

"According to Big Pierre," said DeKok, who had listened carefully.

"I called Headquarters," offered Vledder. "They have a number of tipsters and informers. Most of them are, and wish to remain, anonymous. They didn't know any Manefeldt, or 'Baron', but they assured me, that doesn't mean much. Big Pierre's story *can* be based on fact. According to the Chief of Narcotics, they've had some spectacular successes lately."

"On the basis of anonymous information?"

"Exactly . . . anonymous phone calls."

DeKok looked thoughtfully at his partner.

"If the dealers were being picked up after they had made arrangements with *Monsieur le Baron*, I don't wonder that Big Pierre was worried."

"Uhuh," grunted Vledder. "We *know* that environment. Punishment would, eventually, have to be meted out. Sooner or later they would take revenge." He paused, looked at his colleague. "You want me to check how many dealers have been arrested during the last few months . . . and released? Perhaps there's a clue."

"Yes," nodded DeKok pensively. "Why don't you do that. Pay particular attention to the guys that deal in so-called smoking opium. As you know it's the base for a whole string of drugs, including heroin." With some difficulty he lifted his tired feet off the desk. "Do we still have Jack Stuff?"

"Cell three," declared Vledder. "Tomorrow he'll be brought before the Judge-Advocate."

"For theft of the wallet?"

"Yes. He'll be charged with the hashish at a later date. Narcotics promised they'd take care of it. I'm almost finished with the report regarding the theft."

"Without a complaint? The factual owner is dead."

Vledder smiled cunningly.

"I asked Abigail if she wanted to file a complaint on behalf of the deceased."

"When?" DeKok seemed taken by surprise.

52

"Just now . . . a little while ago. As soon as we came back to the station, *before* I called Narcotics."

DeKok looked at him searchingly.

"The gorgeous Abigail has, I believe, made rather an impression on you." He paused and then added: "By the way, how's Celine?"

"Celine is just fine," answered Vledder brusquely. The sudden mention of his fiancee's name put him at a disadvantage.

"I'm glad," said DeKok blandly. "She's a nice girl." Keeping his young friend further off balance, he returned to the original subject. "What did Abigail have to say for herself?"

"I talked to her myself," answered a momentarily subdued Vledder. "She was very nice. I asked how she was and apologized for your behavior."

"What!?" DeKok was flabbergasted.

"Yes," smiled Vledder, enjoying the opportunity to take a tiny revenge. "You were much too harsh with her and I told her so."

"And?"

"She was going to file a complaint about your behavior."

DeKok snorted. One of the reasons he was always careful to spell out his name, was to make sure it would be spelled right in eventual negative reports, or complaints, about his behavior. There had, over the years, been a number of them. Fortunately, the commendations and praise he had received over the same period of time far outnumbered the negative reports. By now he had so much seniority that he was virtually untouchable. Of course, he *was* a civil servant and would probably never be promoted beyond his present rank. His insubordinate behavior at times, and his unorthodox methods, assured *that*. But neither the Police Department, nor DeKok himself, seemed to be overly concerned with the prospects for his future.

All this flashed through Vledder's mind when he heard his old friend snort contemptuously at the mention of a complaint by Abigail Manefeldt.

"But she did file a complaint against Jack Stuff?" asked DeKok, unaware of Vledder's thoughts.

"Sure. She seems very determined that Jan Brewer goes to jail."

"Determined . . . I wonder why?"

"She was deeply offended," explained Vledder, "when I told her about the wallet. *Whoever robs the dead, is more than a thief*, she said."

DeKok pushed his lower lip forward.

"More - than - a - thief," he repeated slowly. "Perhaps Abigail is right. Perhaps we should have another talk with him. I seem to recall that Jack used to handle opium as well, from time to time."

* * *

DeKok waved in the direction of the chair next to his desk.

"Sit down."

Jan Brewer carefully lowered himself into the chair, pulled up his knobby knees and shivered. He looked bad, pale, with hollow eyes. The stay in the cell had not been beneficial. Nervously he reached for the pack of cigarettes that DeKok pushed toward him. The gray sleuth himself searched for, and found a piece of hard candy that he popped behind his teeth with a satisfied smile. DeKok did not smoke, had not smoked for years, but unlike so many, he did not mind smoking. He used cigarettes as a tool.

"Did . . . eh, did they kill the Baron?" asked Brewer. His voice quavered.

"He was murdered," confirmed DeKok.

"How?"

"Someone gave him a shot of opium."

"Opium," said Brewer, dragging his lungs full of smoke and then again, thoughtfully: "Opium."

"Enough to kill a horse."

"And you think I've done it?" There was a hunted look in the small crook's eyes and he moved restlessly in his chair. "You think I shot him up."

"What do you expect me to think?" DeKok shrugged his shoulders. "You found the Baron at the church wall, *you* were found with his wallet and *you* deal in opium." He spread his arms in a gesture of surrender. "That doesn't leave me much choice, does it?"

"But . . . but I didn't *do* it!"

"I've never met a murderer who confessed immediately." DeKok sounded bored.

"But I'm no killer!" Jan Brewer, alias Jack Stuff, jumped up agitatedly. "I didn't kill him. He was already dead when I found him. I told you so before. I have *always* said that." He sank back in his chair, stretched out a hand to the Inspector. "You know me well enough, DeKok. This isn't the first time you've picked me up. A little stealing, a little blackmail, some fencing . . . all right already. That's how I make a living. But MURDER! That's not my style, DeKok, I wouldn't know how to go about it, I can't harm a fly."

"I know murderers who are afraid of spiders," said DeKok cynically. "What does that prove?"

Jack Stuff clapped his hands to his face. Devastated in the sight of so much uncompromising implacability.

"Oh my God," he wailed, "the Baron was my friend . . . a very good person . . . a real gentleman, the only one I ever met in my whole life."

"So?" snorted DeKok.

Brewer looked confused.

"I did *not* kill him."

"You said that already," sighed DeKok heartlessly.

Jan Brewer lowered his head.

"I want a lawyer . . . a lawyer."

DeKok motioned toward Vledder.

"Take him back to his cell and inform the Public Defender's Office."

Jan Brewer stood up slowly and shuffled out of the room, followed by Vledder. DeKok looked after them, a pensive, calculating look on his face. The conversation had not pleased him at all. There was a gap somewhere, a rift, an unknown factor. Deep down he knew he had failed again. First when he refused to consider foul play and now, during the interview. He had approached the little crook all wrong, had been unable to reach him. For just a moment he considered calling him back, trying to approach the problem from a different direction, using a different manner. Something kept him from putting the thought into action.

Harmen Haaksma, one of the new detectives, entered the detective room with boisterous clatter.

"You're back?" he called from across the room.

"An unnecessary question, don't you think so?"

"The Commissaris has asked for you," grinned Haaksma.

"When?"

"About half an hour ago. He had a visitor in connection with the corpse at South Church. A lady . . . a Mrs. Manefeldt."

DeKok looked up in surprise.

"Manefeldt . . . *Missus* Manefeldt?"

The young inspector nodded easily.

"Sure," he said. "Isn't that possible?"

DeKok rose, scratched the back of his neck and raked his fingers through his hair.

"I have the feeling," he said, clearly irritated, "that *anything* is possible in this case."

5

Inspector DeKok bowed formally while he studied the woman from beneath his bushy eyebrows. He guessed her to be in her early fifties but with a youthful figure. The gray hair was badly dyed and the lips were a little too red. A tawny skin shimmered beneath a thick layer of make-up. He forced himself to look serious.

"Mrs. Manefeldt," he said, "my condolences regarding the loss of your . . . eh, your?"

"Brother-in-law." Her voice was hard.

"Just so," smiled DeKok, "your husband's brother?"

"My *late* husband's brother," she corrected sharply. "Adrian Manefeldt."

DeKok made an apologetic gesture.

"Family relationships are often very confusing for an outsider. You're Abigail's mother?"

"Correct."

The Commissaris joined the conversation. He waved an elegant hand. A red flush colored his usually pale cheeks.

"That . . . is the reason for the lady's presence," he said in his affected voice. "Mrs. Manefeldt has serious complaints to make . . . complaints regarding your attitude toward Miss Abigail, her daughter."

DeKok displayed well-feigned astonishment.

"I have always treated Abigail . . . eh, your daughter, with the utmost respect."

"The lady is of a different opinion," said the Commissaris sternly. "*Positively* of a different opinion. You have insulted her daughter. Have abused her hospitality to . . ."

DeKok tuned out. He was familiar with the litany. He studied Mrs. Manefeldt surreptitiously. The commissarial flow of words passed him by. He reflected that the widow, not too long ago, must have been a good-looking woman of an almost exotic beauty. He imagined the absence of gray in the hair and the removal of the wrinkles around the eyes and came to the conclusion that Abigail had inherited a great deal of her mother's beauty. A smile curled around his lips. Thoughts about Abigail amused him.

When the Commissaris finally ceased talking, he assumed the appropriate expression.

"I'm sorry," he said humbly, "It was never my intention to offend anyone. On the contrary, I found her extremely charming, but . . . I *am* looking for the truth in a mysterious case."

Mrs. Manefeldt reacted furiously. She threw her head back and her dark eyes flashed.

"That's none of our business. It's his own fault. Archibald was never too choosy about his friends. He associated with all sorts of scum. I'm surprised it took so long for somebody to . . ." She stopped suddenly. "I mean, in those circles . . ."

DeKok narrowed his eyes.

"What sort of circles?"

"Do I have to explain that?" She made an irritated gesture. "I would think the police was better informed."

DeKok sighed and abandoned the subject.

"Why did Mr. Manefeldt so often seek out the company of the socially less fortunate?"

"Archibald was part of the Dutch intelligentsia," she snorted. "*An intellectual*, he used to say, *should be close to the people. If he isn't*, he would add, *he's suspect, not to be trusted.* That's why he

58

ignored every vestige of class distinction. He was full of idiotic ideas about the brotherhood of man and that sort of nonsense." She breathed deeply and shook her head in a decisive manner. "Archie was a scatterbrain." It was a definitive conclusion.

"And rich," commented DeKok, rubbing the bridge of his nose with a little finger. "Did he ever use his capital to give substance to his ideals?"

"Archie?" she laughed denigratingly. "Not him, he kept it all to himself. He was a multi-millionaire, but lived like a tramp."

"Are you wealthy?"

"No . . . is that some sort of crime?"

DeKok shook his head slowly.

"I'd be the last to suggest such a thing." He looked at her, scratched the back of his neck. "What about his wife? Did she accept his . . . eccentric behavior?"

She smiled briefly.

"Helen was a dear." There was contempt in her voice. "A small, dear, naive spineless wonder. She didn't have a shred of influence over him."

"You would have been a better wife for him," understood DeKok.

The remark hit its target. Mrs. Manefeldt paled under her make-up. She closed her eyes and her mouth fell open, a hand searched for support on the edge of the desk. The Commissaris was shocked. He approached quickly and led her to an easy chair. As soon as she was seated he poured a glass of water and brought it to her. In passing he gave a DeKok a disapproving look.

"OUT!" he hissed between his teeth.

DeKok left.

* * *

Vledder laughed heartily.

59

"You'll never learn. You have to be nice to the Commissaris . . . nice, cooperative and subordinate."

"I was," growled DeKok with a long face. "Believe me, I have no reason to upset the old man."

Vledder shook his head, chuckling.

"But why did you say, in his presence, that Mrs. Manefeldt should have married her brother-in-law."

"I couldn't help it," answered DeKok, shrugging his shoulders. "It just came out. She was talking so insultingly, in such a contemptuous tone about that 'spineless wonder', Helen, that something inside me began to itch." He grinned boyishly. "I suddenly had the urge to protect the 'spineless wonder'."

"Do you think Aunt Helen was really that spineless?"

"I don't know. I have more the feeling that it was a question of rivalry."

"You mean that they were after the same man . . . in the past?"

"Something like that . . . yes."

"So," remarked Vledder thoughtfully, "Brother Adrian was a second choice, on the re-bound, so to speak."

DeKok's hand roamed through his pockets. After some searching he found a forgotten stick of chewing gum and unwrapped it. He placed the stick, brittle with age, between his teeth and started to chew. Only then did he answer Vledder.

"I don't know," he said, "if that's the right conclusion to draw. Perhaps there are relationships . . . connections we know nothing about." He stuck a finger in his mouth to dislodge a stubborn piece of chewing gum. "Whatever . . . I'm pretty well convinced that Helen received little sympathy from her sister-in-law."

"But didn't Abigail visit her aunt often?"

"Yes," nodded DeKok, "and she speaks with a lot more love about Aunt Helen than her mother."

"Aleida Drosselhoff."

"Is that her name?"

"From German descent," nodded Vledder. "She was married to Adrian Manefeldt, a younger brother of Archibald who died young, at thirty-one. Barely three years after his marriage to Aleida."

DeKok's eyebrows rippled.

"How do you know?"

Vledder, although he had seen the phenomenon more often than most, waited for the display to subside before he answered.

"Simple," he smiled after DeKok's eyebrows had returned to their normal position. "I called the Registry and asked for a complete run-down on Archibald's relatives, even the remote ones. It seemed to be the thing to have available. The family tree is on your desk."

DeKok nodded approvingly. No doubt Vledder had used the computer to come up with some complicated graph. Vledder liked doing things like that. DeKok patted him on the shoulder.

"Poor Adrian," he murmured absent-mindedly, "he was married to a . . ." He did not complete the sentence, but walked over to his desk and sank down in his chair. "Did you ask Headquarters for opium dealers?" he asked.

"They'll look it up," said Vledder. "They'll send it over by messenger. I'm supposed to get a complete list of all dealers in pure opium caught over the last few months." He pushed a chair closer. "Do you expect to find something?"

DeKok gestured vaguely.

"The man, or woman, who administered the lethal injection had a ready supply of water soluble opium." He sprawled more comfortably in his chair and grimaced. "You can't buy that stuff at the drugstore."

Vledder searched DeKok's face while he thought about the remarks of his old mentor.

"You just want the list of dealers," he said with a hint of suspicion, ". . . just to find out to whom smoking opium has been delivered?"

"Exactly."

"So . . . you don't believe in a vengeance killing?"

"Vengeance?" DeKok looked up. "Vengeance from the opium dealers who were betrayed to Narcotics?"

"Uhuh."

"No," DeKok pursed his lips and looked pensive. "No," he continued after a while, "that doesn't seem likely."

"But why not?" Vledder sounded puzzled.

DeKok did not answer at once. He rubbed the corners of his eyes with a thumb and forefinger. It was the movement of a tired man. Vledder watched and, not for the first time, wished he could read his partner's thoughts.

"I think," said DeKok after a long silence, "that they wouldn't have gone to all that trouble."

"How do you mean?"

"If it had been dealers," explained DeKok, "a bullet in the stomach, or a knife in the back would have been cheaper." He grinned bitterly. "After all, opium is their stock-in-trade. Why waste it on a complicated operation like an intracardial injection? Then . . . think about the way the corpse has been manipulated . . . how peaceful and calmly he was resting against the church wall." He spread his arms in a gesture of surrender. "All risks . . . all risks and for what?"

"Symbolism?" offered Vledder cautiously.

"Symbolism?" DeKok laughed mockingly. "Betrayal of opium . . . death *by* opium? Is that what you mean?"

"Yes."

DeKok raked his fingers through his hair, disposed of his chewing gum by flipping it into a trash-can.

"Archibald Manefeldt," he said in a didactic tone of voice, "died because he was a millionaire and *not* because, in his temporary role as Samaritan, he turned in drug dealers to Narcotics."

The phone rang. Vledder picked it up. He listened a few seconds and then replaced the receiver. His face had turned pale.

"What's the matter," asked DeKok, concerned.

Vledder swallowed.

"Jack Stuff has committed suicide in his cell."

* * *

They had placed him on the cot, the strips of shirt with which he had hanged himself, still around his neck. Jan Brewer, aka Jack Stuff.

DeKok leaned forward and looked at the swollen face and the loop that had deeply scored the neck. It was an obvious suicide by hanging. Without a doubt. The remnants of his shirt were carelessly tossed into a corner of the cell. DeKok reached out and closed the eyelids. It was almost a tender gesture. Slowly he came fully upright and let his gaze wander along the dirty walls. He knew the graffiti in the bare cell and he searched for a last word. It was not there. Jack Stuff had departed without farewell. For long minutes DeKok remained at the side of the corpse. His face was serious.

"Everything is free in Heaven," he said softly. It did not sound as a joke, not cynical. And it was not meant that way. DeKok believed fervently that the Lord was merciful, especially toward the souls of small thieves and minor criminals.

Vledder turned toward the Watch Commander, who stood in the door opening of the cell.

"How long has he been dead?"

Bikerk looked at his watch.

"Less than an hour. We looked in on him before the change of the watch."

"Did he say anything?"

63

"Who?"

"Jack Stuff."

"What ... what should he have said?" The tone was suspicious.

"That he planned to do this," gestured Vledder.

The Watch Commander grinned crookedly, pointed a heavy finger at his own chest.

"If I had had the tiniest inkling that he was going to hang himself," he said, excitement in his voice, "then ... then he would never have had the chance. I would have kept a round-the-clock watch on him. If necessary I would have stripped him naked. What do I need with all this hullabaloo? In final analysis, it's *my* responsibility." He paused, looked annoyed, shook his head. "But who figures on that ... Jan Brewer, of all people! ... Dammit, it isn't the first time he's been in a cell. He never caused any trouble before."

DeKok sighed.

"But he did this time ... for the last time."

He turned abruptly and walked into the corridor. Vledder followed.

"What do we do next?"

"Inform his family."

"He has a family?"

DeKok nodded slowly.

"An old mother." At the bottom of the stairs he stopped suddenly. With bowed head he stared at the worn-out steps leading to the detective room. He did not look up for a long time. Then he spoke.

"Get my coat," he said, "I know where she lives."

* * *

She darted busily to and fro, from the room to the kitchen and back again. A small, insignificant old woman, dressed in a roomy housecoat with flowers. Her too large slippers shuffled across the floor. She stopped after entering the room, a happy smile on her face. A sunbeam came through the kitchen window and lit up her gray hair and smoothed out the thousands of tiny wrinkles on her sweet face.

"Lots of sugar, right Mr. DeKok? And what about the young gentleman?" An eagerness to serve, to do something, was in her eyes.

Vledder nodded uncertainly. He was not at ease. He did not feel qualified to bring messages of doom. His tongue stuck to the roof of his mouth.

"A little milk, please," he said hoarsely.

She shuffled away.

The young Inspector looked at DeKok and wondered why he did not tell her at once that her son had hanged himself.

She came back with a pewter tray. With crooked, arthritic fingers she brushed a few invisible crumbs from the table cloth and placed the coffee in front of them. Nice, big cups with a gold border around the rim. She glanced at DeKok.

"You haven't come to see me for a long time," she said pleasantly. "Must have been at least five years. Jantje* has been real good lately." She paused, unsure of herself and tried to read his face. "Or not?"

DeKok ignored the question.

"Does he visit you often?"

"Oh, yes," she asserted with vigor. "At least once a week. Certain! Sometimes he brings me something. When he has money. A few flowers, or a small almond cake." She laughed shyly. "That's my weakness . . . almond cake. But the doctor says I can't have any. Because of the sugar."

Jantje, diminutive for Jan. The Dutch have a penchant for speaking in diminutives by adding "je" or "tje" to almost every other word. They seldom speak of their dog, for instance, but about their "little" dog (hond*je*), even if the animal is a St. Bernard. Similarly with house (huis*je*), car (auto*tje*) and hundreds of other items in daily life, large or small.

"Have you been diabetic long?"

"Years and years," she sighed.

"Do you take medicine, or shots?"

"Injections."

"Does the nurse come for that?"

A happy gleam came into her small brown eyes.

"I'm allowed to do it myself." There was pride in her voice. "Most old people my age ... they won't allow you to do it yourself. Too shaky, you see." She stretched out a hand. "But look at me, steady as a rock."

DeKok smiled.

"I noticed that," he admired, "when you put the tray on the table."

She pushed closer to the edge of her chair and leaned her elbows on the table.

"I've always lived *proper*. No trouble with the Law. I've tried to instill that in *Jantje* from an early age. But when my husband died, it was all over. My Jantje was then just thirteen. A small, skinny boy ... but smart. To provide for the both of us, he went in business ... little as he was. Black market, of course. I don't have to tell you, Inspector, this is a harbor town." She stared into the distance, a tender smile on her face. "But nothing nasty, you understand. Cigarettes ... drink ... watches. All sailors smuggle and they have to sell it to someone, am I right? Well, he made good money and there was no way I could get him back to school. The boy never learned a trade and he can hardly read or write. Business ... haggle ... barter ... dicker ... he has grown up in it. Can you blame him? Sometimes he strayed from the narrow path, I know. He knew no better. When his father died you didn't have all those social organizations. He fell through the net." She sighed, remained silent for a long time. Then she seemed to brace herself and asked: "What do you have him for this time, Mr. DeKok, fencing?"

DeKok shook his head.

"I don't have him anymore," he said somberly.

"Is someone else in charge of the case?" She looked confused.

"You could," DeKok swallowed, "you could call it that."

Her face changed. The expression of sweet tenderness was replaced with sudden fear. Nervously she smoothed out the table cloth.

"What's the matter with Jantje?" Her voice quavered hoarsely.

DeKok chewed his lower lip, looking for words to make her understand.

"I think . . . I think he couldn't face it any more."

She stood up, agitated, restless. Her face became red.

"Face what?"

"Life."

She stared at him as if he had been speaking a foreign language.

"Life?" she repeated.

DeKok nodded slowly.

"We found him in his cell . . . this morning."

It took several seconds before his words penetrated. She sank back into her chair.

"He's dead," she sobbed. "He's dead, he's dead. He's . . ." She repeated it over and over again, shaking her head as if to deny her own words.

Inspector DeKok stood up and sat down next to her. He placed a comforting arm around her shoulder.

"He most certainly must have thought about you during his last moments," he said with conviction. He pressed his lips together and cursed his helplessness, his inability to find more adequate words. Words to comfort her, to console the old woman.

Vledder always maintained that DeKok was so good in conveying bad news to the survivors. He was wrong. DeKok was not good at it. Never had been and never would be. His words were

67

banal, often meaningless. But, realized Vledder in a sudden flash of insight, people sensed DeKok's sincerity, his compassion. The words became simply background noise. It was not what he said, thought Vledder, but the attitude he conveyed.

"I know Jantje loved you very much," said DeKok.

She looked at him with a tear-stained face.

"Why . . . why did he do it?"

DeKok closed his eyes.

"I don't know," he said softly. "I don't understand it either. Jantje had stolen a wallet and that's why he was in the cell."

"A wallet?" There was disbelief in her voice.

"Yes."

She wiped her tears with the sleeve of her housecoat.

"I don't believe that. Jantje isn't a pick-pocket." She shook her head. "Jantje doesn't steal wallets. He's never done that."

DeKok sighed deeply.

"We found the wallet on him and he confessed."

"Who's wallet was it?"

DeKok did not answer directly. He wondered how much he could tell the old woman, how much it would hurt her if she knew the true circumstances. He turned his face away, bit his lower lip.

"The wallet belonged to a dead man," he said reluctantly.

"From a dead man?" There was suspicion in her voice.

"Yes," confirmed DeKok, "Jantje found him against the wall of the South Church and took the wallet."

She shook her head.

"That's not true," she decided. "He would never have done that." She snorted, shook her head again. "From a dead man . . . you must be mistaken."

Suddenly she stood up and went into the kitchen. She came back within a few minutes. She had washed her face and combed her hair. She suddenly looked different, more able, less fragile. It was as if, with her tears, she had washed away her sorrows. She held her head erect, a determined expression on her face.

"Who was the dead man?" she asked sharply.

DeKok gestured vaguely.

"A tramp," he said carelessly. "They called him the Baron."

"The Baron . . . he's dead?" Her face had frozen.

DeKok looked at her searchingly.

"You knew him?"

"He was one of Jantje's friends," she nodded.

"What?"

"A friend." She nodded again. "They used to partner up, from time to time, business you know. He's been here a few times . . . the Baron. A nice man . . . class . . . a gentleman, you could see that at once, despite the rags he usually wore. As a young girl I was a maid in some of the better houses. I don't make a mistake about that. I recognize a gentleman when I see one." She looked at the gray sleuth, a question in her eyes. "How did he die?"

"He was murdered," revealed DeKok.

For several long seconds she was speechless.

"And Jantje has something to do with that?"

DeKok made a sad gesture.

"I can't ask him any more."

She wiped a hand across her face. For just a moment it looked as if she would again burst out in tears. She closed her eyes monetarily, pressed her lips together. Then she recovered. A deep breath escaped her narrow chest.

"Did you know," she said softly, "that they were about to make a lot of money?"

"Who?"

"Jantje and the Baron."

"With what?"

She sighed.

"They were rather secretive about that. I never did find out what it was."

"Did it have anything to do with drugs . . . opium . . . morphine . . . heroin . . . hash?"

She shook her head slowly.

"No, it was something else."

DeKok leaned closer toward her.

"What, then? What was it?"

She made a helpless gesture.

"I don't know."

DeKok placed an arm around her shoulder.

"Please think hard, Mother Brewer," he said in a friendly tone of voice. "It could be very important. Did they say something, anything . . . something you may have remembered? Something that struck you as unusual?"

"I wasn't always there. They would sit together, here, in the room and I was usually in the kitchen. You see, I had the feeling they'd rather not have me around when they were talking."

"Then . . . how do you know they were about to make a lot of money?"

She smiled sadly.

"Last week . . . the Baron had just left . . . Jantje hugged me and said: 'What would you say if I bought you a nice, expensive fur coat?' That's what he said."

"And then?"

She spread her arms wide.

"I said: 'But my boy, you haven't got a penny. You can never pay for that.' Then he laughed and said: 'Ten fur coats, Mother, if you wanted ten of them'." She paused. A tear welled in her eye, dripped down her cheek. With an absent-minded gesture she wiped it away with the back of her hand. "Jantje was a dear boy, sir. He would have bought me that fur coat. Not because I needed it, but because he wanted me to have it."

They remained silent for a long time. DeKok scratched the back of his neck. He had a feeling that the old woman knew more than she realized herself. Something was lurking in her memory, a remark, a gesture, something that could throw new light on the murder that occupied him so intensely. Slowly he stood up, gave the old woman a comforting hug and went to the door. With the knob in his hand he turned back.

"Did Jantje ever go anywhere with the Baron?"

"To where?"

"Anywhere . . .. out of town."

Her face cleared.

"Blaricum," she said decidedly.

"Blaricum?"

She nodded vehemently.

"The Baron wanted that. 'It's about time,' he said, 'that you see my estate.' I heard him say it."

6

"*It's about time that you see my estate.*" Inspector DeKok repeated the words several times, every time with a different intonation "*It's about time that you see my estate.*" He leaned backward in his chair. "A darned remarkable sentence," he observed, "No matter *which* way you look at it."

Vledder seemed less impressed.

"If I were you," he said easily, "I wouldn't see too much in it. More than likely Mother Brewer understood it wrong. She's an old lady."

"Possibly," nodded DeKok with a faraway look in his eyes. "Possibly. But even *if* Mother Brewer was mistaken, for instance . . . if the words had been spoken by her own son instead of the Baron . . . still, it's passing strange."

"Perhaps," laughed Vledder, "Manefeldt wanted to unload his estate on Jantje."

"In exchange for what??

Vledder sighed elaborately.

"Perhaps it was too much for him, after his wife's death. Perhaps he had bad memories about the place. After all, Archibald Manefeldt was an eccentric, all seem to be agreed upon *that*. His actions would certainly have been difficult to predict. Perhaps, he thought it a good joke to pass on the estate to some poor bas . . . eh, a poor person."

"Just like that?"

"Yes."

DeKok grimaced.

"And the poor person is then so happy that he promptly commits suicide?" It sounded hard and cynical.

He stood up from his chair and started to pace up and down the large, busy detective room. His face was serious and deep creases marred his brow. Every once in a while one, or both, of his eyebrows would twitch. He was not at all happy with the case. There were too many gaps, too many blanks, too many strange coincidences. Why did Archibald Manefeldt die and why did Jack Stuff commit suicide? Was there a connection? How and where was the connection? Why did Big Pierre talk about a crusade against drug dealers and why did Mother Brewer assert that the Baron and Jack Stuff . . . a nickname which left little to the imagination . . . were good friends? With what sort of project did they hope to earn a lot of money? He shook his head sadly, avoiding the many obstacles in the room without seeing them. Something did not fit. Did not compute, as Vledder was wont to say. The Baron was rich . . . he did not *need* a lot of money, did not *need* to "earn" it. Most certainly he did not need Jack Stuff as a partner. DeKok grinned to himself. Knowing Jack Stuff assured him that it would probably have been some sort of unsavory business.

He paced for a while, thinking, evaluating, trying theories on himself without coming to a positive conclusion. Suddenly he stopped and stared at Vledder, as usual, busy with his computer terminal. He came closer to the desk.

"Come," he said curtly, "let's hit the road."

The young Inspector rested his fingers on the keyboard.

"Where to?"

"Blaricum. I want to see the estate."

* * *

After a trip fraught with the usual perils of a drive through Amsterdam, such as narrow canal quays, narrower bridges and hordes of bicycles, Vledder reached the outskirts of the city and pulled onto the four-lane highway leading inland toward Hilversum, the "radio" city. All five major Dutch networks are situated there and the town is dotted with radio and television studios and other broadcast facilities, including Radio Holland, the world-wide broadcast service of the Netherlands Government. Blaricum is situated just to the north of Hilversum, within sight of the former Zuyder Zee, now called Ijssel *Lake*. After the massive drainage projects, began in the 1930s, the inland sea had practically disappeared.

As soon as they reached the highway, Vledder took a tighter grip on the wheel. It was peculiar that in the narrow, busy streets of Amsterdam he was completely at ease, drove with a casual, effortless expertise that seemed unaware of his surroundings. When he reached a highway, he became tense, as if forcing himself to stay alert under the relatively stress-free driving conditions. He stole a glance at DeKok.

"I don't understand," said Vledder, "why we're continuing with it."

"With what?" asked DeKok absent-mindedly, sprawled in the passenger seat. He had complete confidence in Vledder's driving and a total lack of interest in the process. He seldom bothered to even look out of the window.

"This case," clarified Vledder.

"I don't understand you," answered DeKok, pushing himself upright in the seat.

"Well, I thought the case was solved."

DeKok smiled gently.

"And who should we arrest?"

"Not necessary." Vledder shook his head. "After Jantje's suicide, we can close the case."

"Jack Stuff?" DeKok sounded surprised.

75

"Yes, I don't know what else you can make of it. His suicide is a clear declaration of guilt, a positive confession. After the last interrogation he must have realized there was no way out. His call for a lawyer was a ploy. The best lawyer in the world would not have been able to get him off. Jan Brewer was cornered. Obviously. Just think . . . he was with the victim on the night of the murder. He was, or could be, in the possession of dissolvable smoking opium. And he could have had a motive because of his relationship with the Baron."

Vledder paused, increased his speed and passed a slow-moving Citroen. There was certain amount of satisfaction for him in the fact that the old VW was able to pass anything at all. After he had pulled back into the curb lane, he continued.

"What occupied me at first," he explained, "was the question of whether Jan Brewer could have accomplished the injection. He didn't use needles himself. I looked at his arms and legs, also between the toes . . . no punctures. He was a hash user and sparingly at that. But when I heard that his Mother was diabetic, performed her own injections, I was convinced. Case solved and closed."

DeKok nodded pensively at the windshield. He did not answer for a long time. It was as if he carefully weighed Vledder's words.

"It's ingenious," he said finally, admiration in his voice. "An impressive summation for the prosecution."

"And?"

"What do you want from me?"

"At the very least a final plea for the defense."

DeKok pursed his lips and searched his pockets. This time he found a peppermint. He idly brushed off some fluff from the white tablet and popped it in his mouth. Vledder glanced at the movement. It was a mystery to him how DeKok was always able to find candy, chewing gum, or other sweets in his pockets. Vledder had never seen him buy any, but he always found something when he went through his pockets. He giggled silently to himself. He had a sudden vision of DeKok as a gray-haired hamster, stashing small stores of candy all over Amsterdam and replenishing his supply from time to time when he came close to one of his secret caches. He pushed the thought aside.

"Well?" urged Vledder.

"You'll have the answer from the defense in due time."

"When?"

"Blaricum," said DeKok, noticing the tall broadcast masts of Hilversum to the right. "Make a left here."

"When?" insisted Vledder.

DeKok looked at him, shifted the peppermint from one side of his mouth to the other.

"As soon as I've found the real killer."

* * *

Vledder parked the VW near the church. DeKok pushed open the door and stepped out of the car. Leaning against the car he looked up at the spire.

"I could get allergic to churches," he said ruefully.

Vledder laughed, thinking his old mentor had made a joke.

"We better proceed by foot from here," he remarked. "Sheep's Lane is rather narrow and it's difficult to get rid of the car."

"Do you have the address?"

"Yes." Vledder consulted his notebook. "Number 79, according to Big Pierre."

"And the key?"

"What key?"

DeKok made an impatient gesture.

"The key to the house, of course."

Vledder looked at him with a puzzled look.

"There's no key."

77

"Forgot it?" DeKok slowed his pace.

"No, no, not at all. There *is* no key."

"Archibald didn't have the key to his own house?" DeKok asked skeptically.

"No." Vledder shook his head. "There was only a key for the abandoned building where he and Big Pierre lived. That was all."

"Then . . . who has the key? Jantje?"

"Him neither." Vledder's face fell. "He only had the key to his Mother's house . . . and a car key.

"A car key?"

"Yes, an old Chevvy. Jack used to sleep in the car, from time to time."

"Where's the car?"

"Still there."

"And where," said DeKok, impatience in his voice, "might that be?"

"Near Count's Gate."

* * *

Sheep's Lane was an old, established, narrow lane with high birches and cobblestones and vague outlines of large houses behind a thick hedge of poplars. DeKok walked in front in his typical, waddling gait, in comfortable slacks and a jacket with patches on the elbows. His hat was pushed to one side, plucks of gray hair peeking from underneath. Vledder followed close behind, appearing almost prim in a neat, gray suit and a narrow tie.

Vledder had no idea what DeKok wanted in Blaricum. What was the use of looking at an old villa? The murder had been committed in Amsterdam. *That* is where they should be looking. The Baron had died there and *there* Jack Stuff had committed suicide. The Baron and Jack had both operated in Amsterdam. He pressed his lips together and cursed inwardly. Why could DeKok not come to the obvious conclusion in connection with the suicide? Jan Brewer had killed the Baron. He had escaped his judges by suicide. It was an obvious conclusion. This trip to Blaricum was nothing but a waste of time. Glumly he pulled a leaf from a poplar.

DeKok halted on the gravel of the wide driveway. He pulled a red, flowery handkerchief from his pocket and wiped the sweat from his forehead.

"This must be the place," he said, panting slightly. He pointed at a weathered post with numbers. "Seventy-nine."

"Well," snorted Vledder, "if we now find the shutters closed and weeds between the tiles, we'll be finished." He sounded sarcastic.

"Finished?" asked DeKok in amazement.

"Yes," nodded Vledder, "then we know as much as what Big Pierre told us yesterday."

DeKok did not react. He pushed the big farmer's handkerchief back in his pocket. His sharp gaze roamed the garden, looked at the neglected bushes, passed over the bolts on the shutters and came to rest on the open window of a dormer. Carefully he walked toward the house. The coarse gravel ground under his heels.

On the big stoop, under an overhang, he stopped. The heavy door now received his attention. Broad, cast-iron studs in the heavy oak gave the door a formidable appearance. He looked up from the large keyhole. A busy spider had covered the top of the door with spider webs. To one side were a number of cocooned flies. DeKok stared at the flies while admiring the intricate webs. He pushed his hat firmer on top of his head. Was there a similarity? What sort of web would he have to weave himself in order to snare Archibald's killer?

He pushed the thought aside. He walked on with a grim smile on his face. Passing the closed shutters, he walked around to the back of the house.

There was indeed grass between the tiles of the patio and weeds had started to creep toward the center of the tiled area. But

DeKok ignored that. He focused his attention on the kitchen door. He knew from experience how simple these locks usually were. People would spend a fortune to protect the main entrance to their house, but neglect the back door, often leaving it completely unlocked. He felt in his pocket and pulled out a small, brass instrument. The instrument had been donated by his friend, the ex-burglar Handy Henkie. With this clever little device DeKok felt confident of opening almost any lock. Vledder looked over his shoulder.

"Do you have a warrant to search the place?"

DeKok looked at him.

"What are you talking about?" he asked with a creditable imitation of total amazement.

"One of these day," sighed Vledder, "you're going to get into deep trouble with that little instrument. It's no less than breaking and entering."

DeKok shook his head.

"I," he lectured, "don't leave traces of my visit."

"Oh yes?" Vledder grinned. "What if they call me as a witness for the prosecution?"

"You'd be an unreliable, hostile witness," answered DeKok with equanimity.

Vledder rubbed his chin. The reluctant, glum expression had disappeared. Suddenly he realized again how much he liked the old man, how much he admired him.

"All right," he laughed, "I'll be an accomplice instead."

DeKok leaned forward, closer to the lock. The lock yielded within twenty seconds. Slowly he turned the knob and pushed open the door. It was not easy. The hinges screeched in loud protest. After the door had been pushed open far enough to allow them to enter, they slinked inside. The kitchen was large and all the walls were covered by cupboards painted in a shrill blue. The faucets were corroded and there was a crack in the granite counter top. A large, old-fashioned coal furnace stood in one corner, underneath a blackened hood. The oven doors were open and missed a hinge. The top of the heavy, cast iron cooking surface was rusted.

"What a mess," observed Vledder.

DeKok replaced Handy Henkie's little instrument in his pocket.

"I think," he scoffed, "that Aunt Helen wasn't your typical Dutch housekeeper." He rubbed a finger along a kitchen shelf. "Dirt," he stated, ". . . and grease."

Vledder who like most Dutchmen had been brought up in a pristine environment, shook his head in commiseration. Dutch houses are generally spotless and housewives will routinely scrub even the pavement in front of their houses with soap and water. The dirt was indeed remarkable. The dust could be explained in a house that had obviously been empty for some time. But dirt . . . and grease . . . it was something to be noted.

"An Aegean stable," said Vledder.

From the kitchen they entered a somber corridor with dark, oak wainscoting and crown molding. A large grandfather clock had stopped at twelve o'clock. To the right they looked into a large, high-ceilinged room with an open hearth, made from rough-hewn stones, dominating an entire wall. There was an overpowering smell of dust, moisture and mold. Carefully DeKok walked past sheathed furniture. There was not much light in the room and he partially felt his way toward the window.

Suddenly he froze. His acute hearing had heard a vague sound from the floor above, a slight movement, a soft thread. He turned around and sped back into the corridor.

He stopped next to Vledder and stared with astonishment at a young man who slowly descended the stairs. He wore a beige, corduroy suit with trousers that were too short and green, suede boots. Tousled blond hair framed his head and a playful smile curled around full, red lips.

"Good morning," he greeted cheerily. "I didn't know I had guests."

The old detective politely lifted his small hat.

"DeKok," he introduced himself, "with kay-oh-kay." He pointed a thumb at his partner. "Accompanied by my colleague, Vledder."

"Sleuths by profession, I take it?" The young man waved his hand in an effeminate way.

DeKok replaced his hat.

"Indeed . . . and . . . with whom do we have the pleasure?"

The young man stopped at the bottom of the stairs and waved at them.

"Archibald, Archibald Vanderwehr . . . more than twenty five years ago I was christened thus in a solemn celebration . . . I was named after my lately so tragically demised uncle Manefeldt."

Vledder was the first to react. He stepped forward with irritation on his face and arrogance in his step.

"What are you doing here?" His voice was sharp, almost hostile. "How long have you been in the house? I've been trying to contact you for some time."

Vanderwehr raised both hands in mock protest.

"I didn't know," he apologized, "that you were looking for me."

Vledder stole a glance at DeKok who remained in the background.

"Your uncle Archibald was a rich man. We're interested in all the heirs."

"Understandable."

Vledder gestured vehemently.

"Nobody could tell me where you were. According to information you have changed address at least four times in the last six months."

"I'm truly sorry," smiled Vanderwehr, "if I've caused you any trouble." His tone was friendly. "But I've never been one to stay long in one place. Besides . . ." He hesitated a moment and then raised three fingers in the air. ". . . three attempts on my life was enough. It seemed beneficial to my health to keep moving around."

Inspector DeKok leaned casually against a wall and listened carefully to the nonchalant tone, the accent, the pronunciation and concluded that the young man had most probably been brought up in the environments of Utrecht, almost in the center of the country. At the very least he had lived there for a long time. Meanwhile he studied the face in more detail: the narrow, straight nose and sharp, pointed chin, the somewhat murky, almost pearly-gray eyes.

"Attempts on your life?" interjected DeKok.

"No less than that." The young man waved negligently.

DeKok detached himself from the wall and gave him a winning smile.

"Suppose you clarify that somewhat," he suggested.

The young man left the bottom of the stairs and walked past the two Inspectors into the room.

"Why don't we sit down," he said resignedly. "Now that you've found me, it might be better if I made a clean breast of it."

"Honesty is the basis of trust," remarked DeKok seriously.

Vanderwehr pulled some of the covering sheets of the furniture and tossed them into a corner.

"Please sit down," he invited, "while I throw some light on the situation."

He walked toward one of the windows. DeKok noticed for the first time that the glass had been broken. Shards were on the floor. From the inside the young man pushed open the shutters and sunlight streamed into the room, coloring everything with brightness. The young man laughed.

"You see, I'm also an accomplished burglar."

He sat down, across from the two cops, with a forced carelessness and intertwined his fingers around one pulled-up knee.

"I've been living here for more than a month," he confessed. "A bit primitive, I must say. In fact, one can hardly speak of *living* in the accepted meaning of the word. It's more camping out ... camping out in the villa of a millionaire." He laughed again, a short, dry, cheerless bark that sounded unpleasant.

"Those attempts ..." pursued DeKok.

Vanderwehr nodded slowly, a shadow fell across his face.

"Ever since Aunt Helen's death," he said softly, "I've had the firm conviction that someone is out to kill me."

"When did Aunt Helen die?"

"Last year ... the third of November."

"You were there?"

"At the deathbed?"

"Yes."

"No, I was informed."

"Who informed you?"

"Aunt Aleida. She was of the opinion that I, as oldest nephew, should consider it my duty to organize the funeral."

DeKok was surprised and showed it.

"*You* were supposed to organize the funeral?"

"Me ... yes."

"And what about Uncle Archibald?"

The young man grinned crookedly.

"He was away on one of his famous roamings. Nobody knew where he was. We tried everything to reach him ... radio, papers, even the Automobile Club. It didn't help."

"So," concluded DeKok, narrowing his eyes, "Uncle Archibald didn't even attend the funeral of his own wife." There was astonishment and suspicion in his voice,

"No ... he wasn't there."

"But, did he hear about it later? I mean ... that his wife had died?"

84

"I can't say." Vanderwehr shrugged his shoulders. "I just don't know. I only know that strange things happened after Aunt Helen's death."

"How's that?"

"First Martha was killed by a car, then . . ."

"Who's Martha?"

"An older lady . . . from here, from Blaricum. Martha . . . I never knew her last name. She used to help Aunt Helen with the housekeeping. Had been doing so for years. As long as I can remember, anyway. She was a big help to Aunt Helen. Uncle Archibald was an eccentric man . . . a bit touched, if you ask me. Aunt Helen, I think, didn't exactly enjoy life with him, she needed support. Just take a look around this house. Everything is old and decrepit. The interior is totally neglected. He never cared about the house, never had any repairs done. And she wasn't *allowed* to call a plumber, or a carpenter. If something broke down, it remained broken. He wouldn't spend a penny on her."

"He spent it on others?"

"No, nobody. He was just a nasty man . . . a braggart, an airhead, who talked about social consciousness, inter-human relationships, understanding among the masses, all that sort of rot . . . but his own wife could go to hell. She hardly had enough money to buy groceries." The young man was obviously getting emotional. "I always felt sorry for Aunt Helen."

DeKok rubbed his face with both hands. Through his spread fingers he peered at the young man, gauging his sincerity.

"Martha was killed by a car," he observed calmly.

"Yes," nodded Vanderwehr. "No doubt it's recorded as a simple accident." His tone was grim. "But as far as I'm concerned it was murder . . . just plain, brutal murder." He moved closer to the edge of the chair, his nostrils quivered and his face turned red. "And the same thing would have happened to me . . . if I hadn't been just a little bit faster." He paused, seemed to recollect himself. It took more than a minute before he went on. "As a pedestrian," he whispered, "you escape death more than once. The Hereafter is closer than you think in today's modern traffic. A step too many, a slight mistake, a tiny error in judgement . . . it's happened before you know it. But . . . if you survive such an experience, you become more alert, more careful, especially the first few days."

Vledder and DeKok nodded agreement. They had seen it happen more than once.

"Well," continued Vanderwehr, "last year I lived in Hilversum, had a job with one of the studios. Everyday, at the same time, I used to cross at a certain corner. One day I was almost killed. It was a matter of millimeters. The car rushed past me so close, I thought it actually brushed me. I cursed the stupid driver and an hour later my legs still shook. Yet, I soon forgot the incident. But the next day . . . the same thing happened again and a week later a third time." He sighed deeply. "I've been lucky. A few bruises, some torn clothes, a scratch or two . . . mostly caused by jumping out of the way." Vanderwehr licked dry lips. "But I soon realized I wouldn't always be so lucky . . . one of these days I would be unable to evade an oncoming car." There was a hunted look in his eyes. "I had to leave . . . away from Hilversum . . . away from that intersection . . . away from cars that came on too fast." he lowered his head. "I've been in flight ever since."

A silence fell between them. Outside the wind played with the new green on the trees. The soft rustling seemed to banish all thoughts of crime. After a long while, DeKok rose and looked down upon the distressed young man.

"So, keeping on the move seemed the healthy thing to do?"

Archibald Vanderwehr looked up searchingly, wondering if DeKok was joking. But DeKok's face was humorless.

"I . . . I feel relatively safe here. Nobody expects to find me here. Everybody thinks the villa is uninhabited, abandoned. I've not been troubled again."

"You went to the police?"

"The police?"

"In connection with the attempts on your life."

"No." Vanderwehr shook his head slowly. "I considered it, obviously. They were clearly murder attempts. But what could I contribute? I mean ... what could I tell the police? I had no witnesses, no proof."

"The license number?"

The young man bit his lip.

"I never was able to see it." He sounded miserable. "I can only say for sure that it was a green Citroen."

"A green Citroen?"

"Yes, you know what I mean, one of those low, flat cars. The front looks like a frog. It has a special hydraulic system."

"A DS21," supplied Vledder.

"Possibly." Vanderwehr's knowledge of cars seemed only marginally greater than that of DeKok.

"What about the driver?"

Vanderwehr sighed dramatically.

"Not the slightest idea. I never was able to catch a glimpse of him."

"Suspicions?"

"Who would gain from my death?" It sounded depressed.

"How about rival heirs?" suggested DeKok.

Vanderwehr sprang up, agitated.

"Other heirs?" His tone was vehement. "There was nothing to inherit. When they tried to kill me, Aunt Helen had just died and Uncle Archibald was still very much alive and nothing pointed toward his immediate demise."

"But in the end," said DeKok cynically, "Uncle Archibald was *also* sped on his way."

"By whom?"

The Inspector leaned closer toward the young man until his face was just inches away from the other's face.

"By somebody," he said softly, threatening, "who had access to smoking opium and who knew how to handle a hypodermic."

DeKok looked at the young man and studied the look in the other's eyes. Then he smiled guilelessly. It was a pose, distracting, confusing. Suddenly, with a flashing movement he took the young man by the left arm and pushed up the sleeve of the jacket. Obvious puncture marks were visible on the bared arm. DeKok grunted.

"Vanderwehr . . . how long have you been shooting up?"

7

They drove back to Amsterdam, Vledder, as usual, behind the wheel. DeKok, also as usual, was sprawled out in the seat next to his young colleague. DeKok despised cars. He was man of slow motions and a melancholy longing for the times of the stagecoach and the canal boats. Life was too fast, he found, too hasty, too superficial. There was no time left for rest, contemplation, thought. Modern man did not live, but was *being* lived. It was a subject he discussed with pleasure whenever he had the time. He grinned at himself. Here he was, complaining about a lack of time and at the same time wanting to discuss the vagaries of modern life *when he had the time*. I'm too complicated for my own good, he thought, not for the first time. Abandoning the subject, he pushed his little hat further down over his eyes and prepared to take a little catnap. Vledder reached the highway and increased the speed of the car.

"A strange bird," he remarked.

"Who?" asked DeKok drowsily.

"Archibald Vanderwehr."

"Strange and dangerous," yawned DeKok. "I watched him rather carefully. The way in which he accepted our sudden appearance showed a certain coolness under fire. Even when I unmasked him as an addict, he kept himself under control."

"You think he's got something to do with the murder?"

"He's certainly involved." DeKok shrugged his shoulders. "Also, he's an opium user. It's a combination that should start us thinking. I'm sure he's fully aware that he makes an almost ideal suspect. It's not at all unthinkable that he enticed Uncle Archibald, one way or the other, to come to the deserted villa in order to administer the deadly injection. It would be a relatively simple matter to place him against the church wall afterwards."

"By himself?"

"No," said DeKok, shaking his head, "that's not likely. The logistics are just a little too complicated for that."

"What if he knocked him out beforehand?"

"Before the cardiac injection?"

"Yes, he could have mixed something in his drink ... a strong sleeping pill, or something like that."

DeKok pursed his lips, thought it over.

"Still," he said after a while, "it remains a formidable task ... for a man by himself."

They drove on in silence. DeKok was now fully awake. Vledder peered through the windshield and chewed his lower lip. DeKok found a toffee in his breast pocket and looked at it with obvious pleasure. He unwrapped the thing and put it in his mouth. He dropped the sticky paper in the ashtray, where it joined a number of similar pieces of paper.

"You know," said Vledder after a long pause, "what I found so strange? Archibald never referred to any other visitors. But, according to what we know, both Big Pierre and Archibald Manefeldt, accompanied by Jack Stuff, must have visited the villa."

"Perhaps," answered DeKok, "he didn't even notice Big Pierre's visit. As far as Jantje and the Baron are concerned, we're not sure if they ever *did* visit the villa together. And if they did, I wonder if Vanderwehr was already living there at the time."

Vledder suddenly burst out angrily.

"By what right does that guy live there anyway?"

"By the right of the bold," laughed DeKok. "you know what they say: *Fortune favors the bold*. Remember, Vanderwehr moved into the villa when Manefeldt was still alive. It's too late to ask him if he objected."

"What about Abigail?"

"As long as the inheritance hasn't been settled, there's nothing much anyone can do. I don't even know if she'd be interested. It would take a lot of money to restore the villa to its former luster. It's totally neglected, the grounds too. I can't figure out why Vanderwehr wants it. It's probably the least attractive part of the inheritance."

"A strange bird," commented Vledder, repeating himself.

"It runs in the family," grinned DeKok. "Archibald Vanderwehr is the only son of the only sister of the late spouse of the ever roaming late Archibald Manefeldt." He grinned again. "If you ask me, Aunt Helen was a bit of a strange bird herself."

Vledder laughed.

"It's a real puzzle. I wonder . . . was Aunt Helen's maiden name Vanderwehr by any chance?"

"Tut, tut," said DeKok. "Have you already forgotten your family tree, the one you made on the computer. First of all, if that were the case, Archibald Vanderwehr would have been illegitimate. No, Aunt Helen's maiden name was Winegarten and Archibald is the son of Henrietta Winegarten. Henrietta married Adelbrecht Vanderwehr, a man from some watered-down nobility."

"Yes, now I remember. They're dead, right?"

"Yes," lectured DeKok, "they've been dead for about five years. Died in a car accident in the Vosges mountains, near Strasbourg. Nephew Archibald is an orphan. After the death of his parents, his Aunt Helen was his closest relative. You see," he added smugly, "you spent a lot of time putting your computer fancies together, but I actually read them."

Vledder accepted the mild rebuke with a smile. He was proud of the fact that DeKok *always*, sooner or later, read what he prepared for him. DeKok had been known to totally ignore the reports from others. Usually he asked Vledder to summarize them if he wanted to know something. It was as if DeKok did not believe it until he had heard it from Vledder, or had investigated himself. It was rather flattering, thought Vledder.

"What about the attempts on Vanderwehr's life?" asked Vledder.

"With the green car?"

"Yes."

"They seem," answered DeKok, pushing himself up in the seat, "incomprehensible. I don't know how to explain them. At first glance they have nothing to do with the case." He paused, scratched the back of his neck. A cynical look came into his eyes. "Unless . . ."

"Unless what?" asked Vledder greedily.

"Unless they worked ahead of schedule," DeKok said simply.

"*Ahead* of schedule?" Vledder did not see the reasoning behind DeKok's thoughts.

"Yes," nodded DeKok slowly, "as a precaution. Knock off all possible heirs, even *before* the benefactor has died. It has happened before."

Vledder swallowed. He was so surprised he almost lost control of the car. The VW took a dangerous slide toward the edge of the road. DeKok did not react in any way, confident that Vledder would recover. He also knew it would never have happened in city traffic. DeKok was not a nervous passenger. Probably because he knew too little about cars to appreciate the dangers.

"That means," said Vledder after the car had been brought back under control, "that Aunt Helen was also . . ."

"Exactly," said DeKok.

* * *

Bikerk, the Watch Commander, looked surprised when Vledder and DeKok entered the station at Warmoes Street.

"Hey," he questioned, "are you two still on duty?"

"From the cradle to the grave," joked DeKok.

Bikerk took off his glasses and stared disapprovingly at DeKok.

"Of course, you didn't have your radio on, so I didn't even bother to call you. I left a message at your house."

"For your information," said Vledder primly, "we were out of town and it was properly logged."

"What was the message," queried DeKok, ignoring the implied criticism of his non-use of modern communication gear.

"There's lady here to see you. She's been waiting for nigh on three hours."

"Three hours?"

"Yes, she came in about three hours ago. I hadn't seen you leave and . . ." He glanced at Vledder. ". . . I neglected to check the car-logs. Anyway, I told her I didn't know when you'd be back."

"Then what?"

"She insisted on waiting." Bikerk sighed elaborately. "I've seldom seen such an persistent person. I tried everything I could think of, but she refused to budge. So, I placed her in the waiting room."

"And she's still there?"

The Watch Commander made a helpless gesture.

"What else could I do? I could hardly put her in the street. We gave her some coffee."

The waiting room in Dutch police stations is a peculiar facility. It is indeed a room where people wait. People in the waiting room are not, technically, under arrest. But nobody ever leaves without official permission. One can smoke, drink, eat, even play cards in the waiting room, but one has to wait, nevertheless.

"Thanks," said DeKok as those thoughts flashed through his mind. "Did she give you any hint what she wanted to see me about?"

Bikerk shook his head sadly.

"Not a word, but she insisted it was very important."

"All right, bring her up in about five minutes."

DeKok climbed the stairs to the large detective room and shortly after he and Vledder had settled themselves behind their desks, a uniformed constable accompanied a woman into the room. He pointed at DeKok and left.

The woman came closer. She walked with some difficulty, as if stiff from sitting too long in one position. DeKok stood up and waited for her to make her way to the desk. He estimated her to be in her early fifties, a large, rather plump woman in a severe suit of dark-brown tweed. She had a round, wide face with friendly eyes that were partially hidden by glasses with a heavy, dark frame. The total appearance was inflexible in some unidentifiable way. DeKok took a few paces forward, meeting her halfway. Suddenly he stopped and stared at the face. He had seen the face before, the characteristics seemed familiar. He hastily searched his memory, but the similarity was fleeting and the association escaped him. Meanwhile she had reached him and he bowed gallantly and led her to a chair. She sank down with a sigh . . . wide, massive, the legs slightly spread.

"You waited three hours?" asked DeKok with his best smile and a tone of amazement.

She nodded slowly, a sad smile around her lips.

"It doesn't matter. I'm used to waiting, hours and hours, in hundreds of theaters, in a thousand dressing rooms. I used to accompany my husband when he was on tour."

DeKok nodded vaguely, listened to the depressed tone she used. He wondered what drove her, why she had asked for him. A lot of women came to the station on a daily basis, usually older women, filled with the most wonderful ideas and preconceptions. They required a lot of time and even more patience. He walked around the desk and sat down behind it.

"You wanted to talk to me," he began carefully.

"You're Inspector DeKok?"

"Indeed . . . with kay-oh-kay."

"They said you would say that," she smiled wanly.

"Who are *they*?"

She waved her hand impatiently.

"People I talked to, about you." She moved in her chair and shook her head. "A few days ago," she said softly, "I read a newspaper article about a dead man who was found near a church. Your name was mentioned in the article."

"That's right."

"Friends told me that I could trust you." She looked up at him. "Has the dead man been identified?"

"Yes," nodded DeKok, "the man's name was Manefeldt . . . Archibald Manefeldt. He's been identified by relatives."

A look of disappointment fled across her face. Slowly she rose.

"In that case," she said unhappily, "I won't bother you any longer."

DeKok looked at her and motioned for her to sit down again.

"You have someone missing?"

"My husband," she admitted slowly.

"Have you reported the disappearance?"

"No." She shook her head. "He's been gone for ages . . . sixteen years . . . last October. The description in the paper

95

sounded familiar. I thought . . . maybe it's him. You see, ever since she left him, he's been on the road . . . a hobo."

"She?"

Her lips quivered.

"That slut," she said angrily, naked hate and revulsion in her voice. She sat down again, the hands clasped in her lap. "One day he told me: *you smother me with your love.* We hadn't been married that long. I took it as a compliment, a sign that he knew how much I loved him. Later I realized it wasn't a compliment at all, but a warning. He meant what he said. My love suffocated him. I loved him so much, I left him no room to live." She worried with a button on her blouse. "One day he told me that he was leaving me."

"With the . . . other woman?"

"Yes." She bit her lip. "She led him to ruin. Took him everywhere, dragged him from one party to another. Ferry started to be late for rehearsals, neglected his work. Then she started to cheat on him. Surreptitiously at first, but quite openly later. Ferry couldn't stand the humiliation, it undermined his self-confidence. He started to drink, sank deeper and deeper . . . until nobody wanted him anymore."

"Then she left him?" asked DeKok.

She nodded imperceptibly.

"As soon as he was rid of her, I went after him, visited him in the boarding house where he lived . . . begged him to come back to me. But he was too proud, preferred to remain where he was." She paused, stared past DeKok with empty, vacant eyes. "For years now," she resumed, "I haven't heard a word about him. I'm not even sure if he's still alive."

She struggled to her feet. DeKok, too, stood up. She stretched out her hand to him and he shook it gently.

"I'm glad you wanted to listen to me," she said. "There are so few people with whom I can discuss it." She smiled, turned around and stumbled away.

DeKok watched her go. Again he had the feeling that he knew the woman, that he had met her somewhere . . . a long time ago. The look, the vague smile, slumbered in the deep recesses of his mind. He frowned. Irritated with himself he again tried to recall the memory. Suddenly . . . there it was, the picture he had tried to form in his mind. He walked after her, overtook her before she had reached the door. Gently he took her by the arm and led her back to his desk, courteously he helped her sit down.

"You are . . .?"

The question surprised her.

"Louise . . . Louise Graaf."

"And your husband?"

"Ferdinand Ferkades."

"Great interpreter of Shakespeare," nodded DeKok.

A happy smile lit up her face.

"You know him?"

DeKok's face fell. Slowly he shook his head. His fingers plucked nervously at his lower lip and let it plop back, a most annoying sound. Vledder watched tensely. It was DeKok's least endearing habit, that and slurping his coffee. With a start DeKok seemed to realize where he was.

"I didn't know him." he said pensively, "not when he was alive, I mean. He was already dead."

A shocked look came into her eyes.

"D-Dead?"

DeKok nodded. He opened a drawer in his desk and took out an old photograph . . . a photograph in sepia tones. The edges were dirty and crushed, the upper right hand corner was missing. He glanced at it and shoved it across the desk toward her.

"He carried it on his heart," he said softly.

* * *

From behind his own desk, Vledder had followed the conversation between DeKok and his visitor. When the woman had left, he stood up and perched himself on the corner of DeKok's desk.

"So, what's our next move?"

DeKok gazed at him calmly.

"Find out the identity of the victim," he said, "it's the thing to do in a murder case."

Vledder missed the sarcasm and gestured wildly.

"But we already know that," he exclaimed. "Archibald Manefeldt. No doubt about it. His papers said so and his niece confirmed it."

"Yes." DeKok nodded slowly. "His papers said so and he's been recognized by niece Abigail."

"And by that business relation," said Vledder, rasing a finger in the air.

"Business relation?" DeKok was surprised.

"Yes," confirmed Vledder, "a Mister Verport. I used him as the second witness."

"Who is Mr. Verport?"

"A broker, an older man. Manefeldt was in business with him some twenty years ago, in Utrecht. That was before the hobo in Uncle Archibald woke up."

"How did you find him?"

"Through Aunt Aleida," smiled Vledder. "At first I wanted to use her as a second witness, but, because of the inheritance question, I decided against it. Therefore I asked her if she knew somebody who was not a relative and would be able to identify the corpse. She mentioned Mr. Verport."

"You never told me."

"But why should I?" Vledder looked perturbed. "The Law specifies identification by two people. Surely that's no secret to you?" A hint of sarcasm came into his voice. "On top of that, the identity of the corpse has never been in question. That's why I don't understand your shilly-shallying with that woman."

"I didn't shilly-shally." DeKok flared up. "It was *her* picture. *Louise, nineteen* it said on the back of the photo. It meant her, Louise Graaf, first wife of the actor Ferdinand Ferkades, aka the Baron, the man who acted out complete scenes of Shakespeare in Lowee's bar in exchange for a couple of beers."

"That doesn't prove a thing," rejected Vledder. "Where does it say that Manefeldt didn't know any Shakespeare? He must have had a thorough education in his younger years."

"Complete with Shakespeare?" snorted DeKok.

Vledder looked determined.

"Why not with Shakespeare?" he asked angrily. "Even I learned his sonnets in school and our class once did a performance of 'Macbeth'." The young inspector paused and took a deep breath. "I think you were a bit . . . a bit precipitous with your conclusions. After all," he said with a certain amount of satisfaction at having been able to apply the sobriquet 'precipitous' to DeKok, " . . . after all, your entire theory is based on one photograph."

"And the difference in character," DeKok said mildly.

"Character?" Vledder's mouth fell open.

"Yes, indeedy," nodded DeKok. "The Baron was a friendly, likeable man and everybody spoke very highly of him. Jack Stuff, Mother Brewer, Big Pierre, all speak about him with admiration. Manefeldt, in contrast, was an eccentric. I haven't heard a good word about him. Not from Aunt Aleida, nor from Nephew Archibald. On the contrary. He was a braggart, an air-head, a scatterbrain who promoted outlandish theories and spouted vague platitudes. He was rich and forced his wife to scrimp and live in a totally neglected house."

Vledder shook his head in despair.

"But you know how subjective witnesses can be. It's all a matter of how you look at it, how long you know a person, what sort of experiences you've had with him. We should stick to the facts . . . and the identifications. Both establish the corpse as Manefeldt."

DeKok pushed his lower lip forward. A stubborn expression dominated his friendly, craggy features. He did not really mind Vledder's arguments. To him it meant that his young friend was thinking on his own. He also knew that Vledder lacked the years of experience that would make him trust his hunches. All that would come with time. Secretly he was proud of Vledder sticking to his guns.

"I take more stock in an old, yellowed portrait," said DeKok, "than a file cabinet full of official papers."

"You're a sentimental old fool," said Vledder, but there was real affection in his voice.

"Ah," said DeKok stoically, "you've accused me of that before."

The young Inspector jumped off the desk and pulled a chair closer. He straddled the chair, resting his arms on the back and his chin on his folded hands.

"Be reasonable, DeKok," he said patiently, trying to convince. "If the dead man at the church wall is *not* Manefeldt, we have to start all over again. There *are* acceptable motives for the murder of Manefeldt. He was a millionaire with greedy beneficiaries as possible suspects. It fits, it computes." He gestured grandly. "Why would anyone want to kill an old, over-the-hill actor?"

"An intelligent question," encouraged DeKok.

Vledder peered at him, cocking his head quizzically.

"You really believe the dead man was Ferdinand Ferkades?"

"I believe," answered DeKok pensively, "that we should not exclude the possibility."

"Well," swallowed Vledder, "if you're right . . . then . . . what happened to Manefeldt?"

DeKok stood up and ambled over to the coat rack, a smile on his lips.

100

"We'll have to ask niece Abigail," he told Vledder.

8

"Where is Uncle Archibald?"

Abigail stared at the gray sleuth with astonishment in her eyes.

"I . . . I don't understand you."

"Where is Uncle Archibald?" repeated DeKok with a friendly smile.

The young woman's face froze into disapproval.

"An indecent question . . . don't you think so yourself? As far as I know Uncle Archibald was never very religious. He never went to church. It's seems a bit odd to discuss the salvation of his soul."

"We're in no position to form a judgement about that," said DeKok diffidently. "Happily that's not our concern. In any case," he continued, "it might be a bit premature."

"What *do* you mean?"

DeKok did not answer at once. He wondered if Abigail had misinterpreted his question on purpose. What sort of game was she playing? He smiled to himself. Did she really think he was interested in the state of Uncle Archibald's soul?

"Did you love your uncle?"

She forcefully shook her head, causing the blonde hair to fan around her head.

"He was a nasty man," she said with conviction. "When I was still a child he always used to chase me with spiders and dead mice. He knew I was terrified of them." She paused, shoved the hair from her face. "It's a long time ago, but sometimes I still have nightmares about it."

"You didn't like to go to Blaricum?"

"Mother always insisted that I spend my vacations there." She shrugged her shoulders. "And Aunt Helen was a dear soul. She protected me as much as possible. But she could not defend me against Uncle's teasing. He had devilish tricks."

"Devilish?"

"He used to haunt the place at night." She bit her lower lip. "Just for so-called fun . . . he'd pretend to be a ghost, to frighten us. Once I ran away, clear across the heather, in just my nightdress."

"And yet your mother insisted you go there?"

"Mother wanted to make sure I would be in the will." She smiled sadly. "She used to say: *They've no children of their own. If anybody is entitled to the money, it's you.* It was an article of faith with her."

"Is that so?"

"Yes, she said it." Her gaze wandered.

"But," feigned DeKok, "doesn't nephew Archibald have the same rights?"

"I suppose so."

"Have you ever met him?"

"Just once. About six months ago. At Aunt Helen's funeral."

"Did he never spent a vacation in Blaricum?"

"He wasn't allowed."

"Who didn't allow it?"

"Uncle Archibald. *I don't want your idiotic family in this house.* I heard him say it often enough."

"To Aunt Helen?"

"Yes. They used to quarrel about it."

DeKok rubbed the bridge of his nose with a little finger. Then he put his hand in a pocket, as if looking for some candy, seemed to think better of it and scratched the back of his neck instead. Meanwhile he glanced around the room as if he had forgotten all about Abigail. Suddenly he turned his face toward her.

"Who told you to identify the dead man as Uncle Archibald?"

"Mother." She sighed deeply. It did exciting things to her chest, but DeKok did not notice.

"Mother?" he urged.

"Yes. She had read the newspaper article and told me to go have a look. *I bet it's Uncle Archibald*, she said."

"And?"

She looked at him, incomprehension on her face.

"What do you mean?"

"Did you find him changed much?"

She lowered her eyes. Her tongue darted out and licked her lips. It was an unconscious, highly erotic movement.

"I . . . I thought it was rather icky," she whispered. "I'd never seen a dead person before. I was afraid . . . I didn't really dare look."

"So . . ." DeKok leaned toward her. ". . . you did *not* recognize him." It was not a question, but a statement. His tone was severe.

She jumped up, suddenly she changed her attitude, her tone of voice. Her face became red. She stared at DeKok with wide, frightened eyes.

"Yes," she cried out. "I *did* too recognize him! Yes! It *was* Uncle Archibald!"

* * *

After the heavy door had closed behind them, they walked from Count's Gate toward Prince Henry Quay, Vledder in front, glum, lips pressed together. DeKok followed a few feet behind, almost strolling, a thoughtful look on his face. The old sleuth did not feel right. The investigation was not going as he wished. The conversation with Abigail had not satisfied him. Had she indeed recognized the corpse as her uncle? Or had she lied? But why? What was the sense of it all? Why would she identify a total stranger as her uncle . . . a man who happened to be murdered? A strong feeling of uneasiness overcame him, gnawed at his equanimity. The old portrait bothered him. *Louise, nineteen*. Was he truly a sentimental old fool? He looked at Vledder who had suddenly stopped.

"I think we should ask some more questions of Verport," suggested DeKok.

"He's a reliable person," objected Vledder. "I *did* check his credentials."

""Perhaps, but he hadn't seen Manefeldt for over twenty years."

Vledder became touchy, partly because he was beginning to share DeKok's misgivings.

"Do you mean to imply that I handled the identification wrongly? That he fooled me?"

DeKok placed a fatherly hand on the young man's shoulder and shook his head.

"You know better than that. I just want to suggest that both Mr. Verport and the lovely Abigail *could* have been mistaken . . . did not take a close look at the corpse. It didn't have to be deliberate. Perhaps a certain amount of predilection."

"A what?"

"Predilection," grinned DeKok, ". . . subtle influence . . ."

Vledder looked puzzled, trying to make the connection.

"You mean," he said slowly, "that someone suggested they would see Manefeldt and therefore they *did* see Manefeldt?"

"Something like that . . . yes."

"Hypnosis?"

"Nothing as dramatic as all that," said DeKok, "there are other ways to influence people, to make people believe that they will see what they expect to see."

He stopped suddenly. Both man watched a car turn sharply off Prince Henry Quay toward Count's Gate. It was a low car with a flat nose. The car stopped with screeching tires in front of number thirty-seven. A man stepped out and slammed shut the door of the car.

"Raymond Verbruggen," observed DeKok.

"In a green DS21," supplied Vledder.

* * *

"Martha Noyes."

DeKok looked up absent-mindedly.

"Who might that be?"

Vledder tapped the screen of his computer with a pencil, checked some scribbles in his notebook and turned toward DeKok.

"Late in the evening of seventeen November last year, she was found unconscious and with severe head wounds on the road between Blaricum and Hilversum. Her crumbled bicycle was found in a ditch about twenty yards away. She died in the ambulance without regaining consciousness, before she reached the Emergency Room in Hilversum."

"Aunt Helen's faithful retainer."

"According to police reports she had been visiting an old friend in Hilversum and was on her way back to Blaricum. She visited her friend every Thursday night and then went back to the old farm she shared with her invalid sister on the outskirts of Blaricum."

"Any signs of a crime?"

"Hit and run. The remains of the bicycle were investigated by the Hilversum police and there were traces of green car lacquer on the rear fender of the bicycle. Somebody had come up to her from behind."

"Scuff marks? Signs of braking?"

"No."

"How about down the road? Any sign of the driver stopping to investigate?"

"No."

"What else?"

"Nothing else." Vledder made a helpless gesture. "An APB went out with the request to apprehend the driver of a green car with a damaged right front fender." He glanced at the screen, quickly clicked from one screen to another. "It was all a bit vague," he continued, "and there were no results. Martha Noyes was buried three days later in Blaricum, the local pastor did the eulogy, praised her loyalty and sacrifice. *Martha . . . Martha . . . thou art careful and troubled about many things . . .*"

DeKok stared at his young colleague with astonishment.

"That's in the police report, that's in the computer?"

"No," laughed Vledder, shaking his head. "It's from the New Testament, Luke 10:41, according to the Blaricum constable who attended the funeral. Apparently he's a very religious man and remembered the text. He had known Martha for some years and he and Martha belonged to the same church. He found the pastor's text very appropriate."

DeKok stared into the distance, pulled his lower lip and let it plop back. He was deep in thought and repeated the annoying gesture and its accompanying sound several times.

"Well," he said finally, "what it comes down to, without all the ruffles and flourishes, Vanderwehr was right . . . it was murder."

"Maybe not," interjected Vledder. "The Blaricum police are thinking in terms of an inexperienced, or drunk driver. That would make it manslaughter. Murder does not seem likely. Martha Noyes had no enemies and was generally respected and liked."

"What happened to the invalid sister?"

Vledder looked sad.

"The farm was sold at a fire-sale price and the sister went into a nursing home."

"Where?"

"In Bussum."

"You have the address?"

"No . . . why?"

"Find it. Invalids often have a long time to think."

The phone rang before Vledder could comply with the request. He lifted the receiver and listened. After a few seconds he replaced the instrument in its cradle and looked at DeKok. His face was serious.

"The Commissaris wants to see you."

DeKok rose with some difficulty, grimaced and left the room.

* * *

Inspector DeKok entered without knocking. He stopped, surprised, the door knob in his hand. Aleida Manefeldt was sitting in an easy chair next to the window. She wore a navy-blue suit and a hat with a veil. Her dark eyes flashed behind the tulle of the veil.

The Commissaris was seated on a similar chair next to her. His face was red and flushed. He wiped the sweat from his forehead with a white handkerchief. DeKok grinned to himself. Apparently a heated discussion had preceded his entrance. Softly he closed the door behind him an entered the room. The Commissaris waved toward an empty chair.

"Sit down, DeKok," he said with his frog-in-throat voice. "I have to speak seriously to you. Apparently you ignored my last warning." He indicated the woman. "Mrs. Manefeldt has again approached me with complaints about your behavior. She considers your actions in regards to her daughter scurrilous and unacceptable."

DeKok raked fingers through his hair.

"Murder, too, is scurrilous and unacceptable."

The Commissaris pressed his lips together in an attempt to control himself.

"Of course," he said after he felt he could trust his own voice again, "but that does not give you the right to approach those involved in a discourteous manner."

Mrs. Manefeldt leaned forward.

"We're *not* involved," she said sharply. "We don't have anything to do with Archibald's unfortunate death. Your Inspector is looking in the wrong direction. He should look in the environment where Archie spent most of his time ... tramps, addicts, outlaws." She moved restlessly in her chair. "We have no objection if reasonable questions are asked in the proper manner, but we refuse to accept unfounded accusations."

"Did I do that?" asked DeKok guilelessly.

Mrs. Manefeldt lifted her veil. Her dark eyes flashed as she raised an admonishing finger in the air.

"I *forbid* you to ever again approach my daughter without my being present." She spoke rapidly, emotionally. "I have given her strict instructions to answer no more of your questions." She paused to catch her breath. "And the next time you find it necessary to visit her in her house at Count's Gate, I'd advise you to have an authorizing warrant with you. I have instructed Abigail not to let you in without it."

"But why? Do you have something to hide?"

Mrs. Manefeldt swallowed. Her face became redder.

"We do not appreciate your visits. We further wish to be spared your insinuations. My daughter Abigail is a sweet and gentle child ... too sweet and too gentle to be subjected to your blunt, obnoxious interrogation methods. To be ... to be ...."

"... to be damaged by them?" completed DeKok.

"Exactly!" She nodded vehemently. "To be damaged."

DeKok rubbed his face.

"Is Abigail your only child?"

"Yes."

"Did you pick the name 'Abigail'? I noticed that the name doesn't appear anywhere else in your family. You know what the name means?"

"I know . . . yes."

DeKok made an inviting gesture toward his Chief.

"Perhaps you'd like to tell the Commissaris? Probably he doesn't know the meaning of the name."

Mrs. Manefeldt hesitated. She adjusted the collar of her blouse. Her arrogant demeanor evaporated, her determination seemed to disappear.

"Abigail means . . . *father's joy.*" Her voice trailed away.

DeKok nodded agreement.

"*Father's joy,*" he repeated pensively. "The joy, or happiness, of the father. Abigail was born exactly two hundred and ninety days after your husband died. According to my information, your husband was seriously ill for several months *before* his passing. Adrian Manefeldt was ill enough that the . . . eh, the sex act was out of the question." DeKok paused briefly and leaned toward the woman with an interested look on his face. "Mrs. Manefeldt," he inquired politely, "Abigail was the joy of *which* father?"

The woman looked at him with frightened eyes. All the blood drained from her face and her gaze wandered away. Suddenly she collapsed against the back of the chair. Her hands fell from her lap and her hat balanced precariously on one ear.

Slowly DeKok stood up and looked down at her with cold, unaffected eyes. The Commissaris rushed toward the water cooler. With the paper cup already in his hand, he gave DeKok a scorching look.

"OUT!" he roared.

111

* * *

Vledder gave DeKok a perplexed look.

"Two hundred and ninety days? But isn't that a bit long? I always thought that a normal pregnancy lasted about two hundred and *eighty* days."

"Nine months," confirmed DeKok calmly. "The Law, however, recognizes a term of three hundred days. According to our Laws, a child, born within three hundred days after the dissolution of marriage, for whatever reason, death or divorce, is considered to be an issue from that marriage. There was nothing illegal about Abigail being named a Manefeldt. But as I studied the family tree, I could not help but think there was something wrong with the way Abigail was conceived."

"Why?"

"In the first place, the two hundred ninety days. That was long, as you so rightly observed. Also, Adrian Manefeldt died of cancer of the bladder and was in a coma for at least four weeks *prior* to his death."

"He could not have fathered the child."

"Exactly. And then I wondered why a child, that was not the result of intercourse with the lawful father, was called Abigail . . . *father's joy?*"

"Yes," smiled Vledder, "under the circumstances it is indeed a strange choice for a name. Would she have thought about it? Perhaps she just picked it because she liked the name?"

"No, of course, she thought about it. She knew full well what the name meant. It was deliberate."

"In order to upset the real, I mean, the *natural* father?"

"As a constant reminder to the father that *he* was the father." He scratched the back of his neck. "You see," he went on, "something Abigail said in our last conversation struck me as curious. She told us that her mother would insist she spent her

112

holidays in Blaricum. *If anybody is entitled to the money, it's you*, her mother used to say."

"You mean . . ." hesitated Vledder.

". . . that *Archibald*, not Adrian, was Abigail's father," supplied DeKok. "You have it in one!"

* * *

DeKok swept his hat off his head, held it against his chest and made a leg. Somehow it did not look awkward, but a natural gesture by a person transported from another age.

"DeKok . . . with kay-oh-kay . . . professional sleuth."

Maria Noyes smiled and pointed to the side.

"Then he must be Vledder," she said, amused.

DeKok nodded and pressed the hand she stretched out toward him. The hand was long, slender and as white as marble. A friendly nurse shook up her pillows and disappeared without a sound. The room had modern furniture with a touch of refined luxury.

"You like it here?"

"It's all very nice and they're really kind to me," she said, glancing around. "But I often think of our little farm and of Martha. She was always so helpful, so strong, so sure of herself. I owe her a lot. She's been taking care of me ever since our mother died. And that's quite a long time."

"She earned a seat in Heaven," said DeKok, looking intently at her pale face.

"The pastor said that I have gotten the better deal." Her face fell and there was doubt in her voice. "But without Martha I wouldn't have survived this long."

DeKok nodded to himself.

"Martha was *careful and troubled about many things*," he quoted.

"You know the Bible?" she asked happily.

"I know what the pastor said during his sermon at the grave."

113

"Since I've moved in here," she said, smoothing the blankets, "I've thought a lot about Martha's death. The police said it was an accident . . . a drunk driver, or something like that . . . but I don't believe it." She closed her eyes monetarily. "She's been murdered."

"Why?"

"She knew too much."

"About what?"

"Strange things happened at Sheep's Lane." There was a haunted look in her eyes.

"In the Manefeldt villa?"

"Martha was very upset the last few weeks before her death." She nodded to herself, her face was serious and a corner of her mouth quivered. "I noticed it, of course. She started to forget things and that never happened before."

"Aunt Helen's, I mean, Mrs. Manefeldt's death must have touched her deeply." He gestured. "It *was* rather sudden."

"No, no." She shook her head. "Martha had expected that. *The pour soul won't last much longer, she runs screaming through the house.* That's what Martha said."

"Screaming through the house?" repeated DeKok, lifting a single eyebrow.

"She suffered from nightmares. She almost never slept. She saw ghosts everywhere."

"Ghosts?"

"Yes. One time she came to us in the middle of the night . . . an old coat over her night dress. She scared me that time . . . she looked terrible."

"When was that?"

"About ten days before she died."

"Then what happened?"

"Martha got dressed and took her back to the house. She didn't come back until late the next day, completely upset. *Maria, don't you think that a person is entitled to a Christian burial?*

114

That's what Martha said." She paused, again smoothed out perfectly wrinkle-free blankets. "I thought about it. You see, because of religious considerations, we're against cremation. The resurrection, you see. We . . ."

DeKok interrupted impatiently.

"Who was supposed to be entitled to a Christian burial?"

She placed the back of her hand against her forehead.

"I've been wondering about that for months. I don't think Martha was talking about cremation at all. It had to do with something that happened at the villa."

"What happened at the villa?"

Maria Noyes avoided his eyes, she moved restlessly in the bed and shook her head. There was an uncertain, confused look on her pale face.

"*Young* Archibald asked the same thing."

"He's been here?" asked DeKok with genuine amazement.

"Yes," she nodded. "He came to express his sympathy about Martha's death. He was very nice, very kind . . . understanding, you know. He said that Martha had always been a big help to his aunt and that Uncle Archibald was sure to express his gratitude in more tangible form. Martha had earned a well-deserved rest after her busy life, he said, and it was extremely sad that she had been taken away in such a terrible manner."

"And then he asked what had happened at the villa?"

"Not directly." She swallowed. "He said that his aunt had always trusted Martha completely and that they had no secrets from each other."

"In short," grinned DeKok, "he wanted to know what sort of secrets *you* knew."

"Exactly," she nodded. "But I told him that I knew nothing that she never told me anything, that Martha wasn't very talkative by nature." She looked up at the gray sleuth. "And she wasn't, you know." Suddenly she spoke sharply, agitatedly. "Martha was a bit withdrawn, with a strong, self-sufficient character. She'd be th ideal type if you wanted an accomplice to help kill ..." She stopped suddenly, frightened by her own words. Her eyes almost popped out of their sockets as she stared at DeKok. Abruptly she turned around and hid her face in the pillows. "No, no," she sobbed, the sound smothered by the cushion, "not Martha ... *not* Martha!"

DeKok stood up and looked down at her. Then he turned toward Vledder. The young Inspector looked pale. DeKok went over to the window and gazed out over the gardens. The lawns had been freshly cut and there were a lot of yellow tulips and forsythias.

Suddenly he visualized the neglected garden of the villa, the grass and weeds between the tiles of the terrace, the decrepit, filthy kitchen in clashing blue, Nephew Archibald and the sheathed furniture. What sort of drama had happened there? Behind him he could hear Maria's sobbing.

"Has Aleida been here as well?"

The sobbing stopped. Maria lifted a tear-stained face from the pillows and looked at him.

"The witch!" There was revulsion in her voice, revulsion and hate. "A tool of the Devil ... she, she and her Belgian ... *gentleman*." The last word sounded like an indictment.

"Belgian gentleman?"

"Yes, that ... that Raymond, whatever his name is. They came to visit me at the farm. Martha hadn't been buried yet, the coffin was still next door. They wanted to know if Martha had taken away any jewelry." She started to cry again. "Jewelry! As if Martha would do such a thing!" She swallowed her tears, her hand went to the bedside table, groping for a tissue. Vledder hastened to push the box closer to her. "Aleida," she continued after awhile, a hard look on her face, "roamed the villa for days after old Mrs. Manefeldt died, looking for things. Finally young Archibald sent her packing."

DeKok's eyebrows rippled suddenly, wildly. The display seemed to freeze both Maria and Vledder as they watched with spellbound fascination.

"Did anybody ever ask after *old* Archibald?" asked DeKok as his eyebrows came to rest.

"But why?" she asked with genuine amazement. It was not certain whether she was surprised at the question, or about the incredible antics of DeKok's eyebrows. "After all," she went on, "he was roaming about . . . everybody knew that."

DeKok gave her his best smile.

"Of course, I had forgotten." He took his little felt hat from the bed and bowed over her hand. "We'll come and visit you again, some other time. You'll be here for the time being?"

"Until it pleases Our Dear Lord to take me away," she said softly and with simple faith.

9

DeKok placed both legs on his desk. The familiar little devils that always plagued him when a case was not proceeding according to plan were again at work. When he was at a dead-end, searching in the wrong direction, his legs and feet would hurt. It was an unfailing barometer of his progress. Normally he could walk tirelessly. His typical, somewhat waddling gait was familiar to most people in and around Warmoes Street station. But only a few people knew about the pain that sometimes just about disabled him. Vledder was one of those few and he peered unhappily and with concern at his old friend, careful not to say anything, because DeKok was also highly irritable in this state.

DeKok, in an effort to banish the pain of a thousand little devils with red-hot pins that seemed to be putting in overtime on his lower extremities, reflected on what they had learned so far. It was not much and most of it negative. The connecting link was missing. The how and the why remained a mystery. What was Martha's role in the scheme of things? What did she know? And who was the person for whom she posed a danger? A danger so real, that murder was the only solution? What had happened in the villa? Why was Aunt Helen so afraid that she fled into the night? Ghosts? Nonsense! Was her conscience bothering her? With a disgusted look on his face he threw a pencil on his desk.

"Question! Questions!" he exclaimed. "Nothing but questions! There *has* to be a connection somewhere." He slapped his hand flat on the desk. "Darn it," he added with his most powerful expletive, "it's almost as if I've forgotten how to think!"

Vledder pushed a chair closer to DeKok's desk.

"Why don't we arrest Raymond Verbruggen?"

"On what grounds?"

"Murder, of course. The murder of Martha and his attempts on the life of Archibald the younger."

"Aha, the green car and the slivers of paint on the bicycle."

"Exactly."

"That's the problem, you see," explained DeKok, raking his fingers through his hair. "We'd first have to find out how long he's had the car and if he's ever been in an accident with it. Otherwise you don't have a leg to stand on." He grimaced, thinking of his own painful legs. "How many cars of that type are there? Also, what could possibly be his motive?"

"That's easy," grinned Vledder. "The interests of Abigail . . . his intended."

"I grant you that. It could serve for the attempts on Archibald. But what could be his motive for wanting to kill Martha Noyes?" He paused and looked thoughtfully into the distance. "Did they analyze the car paint in Hilversum, or Blaricum?"

"I don't know," said Vledder, shrugging his shoulders.

"Well, find out. If it hasn't been done, ask them to do it. It may come in handy. Whoever silenced Martha forever . . ." He stopped as the door at the far end of the large detective room suddenly opened and a strangely dressed figure became visible in the door opening.

The man wore tight jeans with patches, a black shirt and a fur jacket. He closed the door behind him, turned to the nearest detective and asked a question. The detective pointed across the room toward Vledder and DeKok. The man lifted the heavy suitcase he was carrying and approached DeKok's desk. He placed the suitcase on the floor in front of the desk and grinned broadly at the two Inspectors.

"You . . . you're not getting anywhere, are you?" It sounded disapproving. "I mean, you haven't caught him yet, the murderer of the Baron. I buy a paper everyday, just for that, to find out if you've done your job."

DeKok looked serious.

"You were his friend. Big Pierre and the Baron. You even have a nameplate to that effect on your door. *You* have spent the last three months with him. We sort of hoped that you would have a few important hints for us."

"Me?" Big Pierre laughed sheepishly. "Me? I told you where you could find the killer. The dealers weren't at all fond of the Baron."

DeKok looked like he did not believe a word of it.

"He was quite friendly with Jack Stuff."

"That's different," grinned Big Pierre. "The Baron was using Jack." He pushed the suitcase closer to the desk and sat down on the chair across from DeKok. "You see, Jack was just a little guy, not a real dealer. He haggled a little, traded a little, kept a small percentage. You've got them by the hundreds. He just wasn't *really* big. No, he wasn't. But . . . he *did* have a lot of contacts."

"And the Baron used those."

"Exactly. Jack could lead him to the big guys, people who process and distribute to the smaller dealers, you see. As you know, a lot of it comes in as uncut opium and has to be processed into heroin and other stuff. That takes money, laboratories, really big people, people who don't think in ounces, but in kilos."

"And were they on the trail?"

"I thought so." Big Pierre spread his arms in an expansive gesture. "They'd been working on it for some time." He smiled. "Jack even thought it would make him rich."

"How?"

"They didn't tell me everything," sighed Pierre. "Besides, I didn't *want* to know everything. It was a little too dangerous for my blood. Look, my philosophy is, if you want a joint, a trip, or a shot, you buy it, you see. Just like that . . . if you got the dough. Otherwise . . . nothing."

"Were they thinking in terms of betrayal? Bribes? Tip money from the police?"

"Tip money from the police!" Pierre snorted. "That will never make you rich." He shook his head. "No, it was something else. The Baron even grew a moustache for it."

"A moustache?"

"Yep, a big, droopy moustache."

"What was the use of that?"

"I don't know." Big Pierre shrugged his shoulders. "He had to look like somebody, I think. The guy that was supposed to take delivery. I wasn't all that interested. I *did* warn them, though. I knew how it would end: with - your - dead - back - against - a - cold - wall . . ."

He stared sadly at the floor, a tear in the corner of one eye. His fingers stroked the "ban-the-bomb" symbol on his chest. After a long pause he pointed at the suitcase.

"I've a new roommate . . . somebody from the same province as myself, from Friesland. We speak Frisian together. This is the Baron's suitcase. Perhaps his nephew has a use for it. It's just in our way."

DeKok gave him a searching look.

"Nephew?" he asked.

Big Pierre smiled knowingly.

"The Baron has a nephew. Didn't you know that? I met him in Blaricum."

"When?"

"A few days ago, at the villa."

"What were you doing there?"

122

"Just looking around." He waved vaguely. "Just to see what sort of vultures had gathered to divide the carcass."

"And you met the nephew?"

"Yes," nodded Pierre. "I was in the garden and he saw me, wanted to know what I was doing there. I told him I was a friend of the Baron and he looked sort of strange at me, as if he didn't understand me. 'A friend of the former owner,' I explained. Then he asked me if he called himself the Baron and I said 'yes' and he laughed. Then he asked me to come inside. We talked for a while and he showed me around. I told him he should do something about the place. 'Open the windows and the shutters,' I said, 'or everything will rot away.' Then he laughed again and said that it might be best. Apparently he doesn't like that beautiful house very much." Again Pierre pointed at the suitcase. "I could take it to Blaricum myself, I suppose, but it's a bit heavy and I don't have a car."

He looked at DeKok, waiting, as if expecting the old cop to say something. DeKok asked no further questions, but merely stared at him. Pierre moved in his chair and finally stood up and walked away. After a few paces he stopped and turned around.

"I guess I'll hear about it when you catch the killer," he said as he proceeded again toward the door.

"I'll come and tell you personally," promised DeKok toward his retreating back.

Pierre raised a hand in acknowledgement and left the room.

Vledder lifted the heavy suitcase on top of his desk and lifted the lid. The contents were pathetic. Dirty underwear, a black sweater with holes, an old hat and a discolored jacket. The young Inspector lifted the garments out of the suitcase between thumb and index finger and one by one dropped them on the floor. An old chest, wrapped in dirty rags, next caught his attention. DeKok came to stand next to him.

"A make-up case," he ascertained.

Vledder opened the case. Sticks of greasepaint spilled out and rolled across the desk. On the inside of the lid, to the right of a mirror, they found the photo of a man, a man with a large, droopy moustache.

Vledder smiled in surprise.

"The Baron."

DeKok shook his head.

"Uncle Archibald," he corrected.

* * *

"What do you want to do with these old rags?"

"See if someone recognizes them."

"Like who?"

DeKok scratched the tip of his nose.

"Louise Graaf," he said." He gave a creditable imitation of her husky voice: "*I'm used to waiting, hours and hours, in hundreds of theaters, in a thousand dressing rooms.*" He laughed at his young partner. "Believe me, she'll know her husbands's makeup case."

"Ferdinand Ferkades," said Vledder and had the grace to look abashed.

"The man who was supposed to look like Archibald Manefeldt ..." confirmed DeKok, unwittingly rubbing salt in Vledder's wounds. He hesitated, pointed at Vledder and added: "... and *did* look like him so much that both Niece Abigail and your Mr. Verport identified him as such without any hesitation."

Vledder raised his hands in mock despair.

"But why?" he exclaimed. "What was the sense of that masquerade?"

"In some ways," said DeKok languidly, "there are certain advantages to impersonating a millionaire. Remember what Big Pierre said. Jack Stuff was convinced he'd soon be rich."

124

"And promised his mother a fur coat." Vledder smiled bitterly.

DeKok agreed sadly.

"Ten fur coats, Mother, if you wanted ten of them," he quoted Jantje. He bit his lower lip and continued. "Jack and the Baron were after something big ... a colossal caper. Manefeldt's millions formed the stake. Their trip to Blaricum and the Baron's remark about it being time Jack saw his estate, are all indications toward that."

"But how?" questioned Vledder.

"Perhaps they intended to draw money out of his bank account. That seems the most obvious. I'm sure their thoughts went that way. After all, they had Manefeldt's papers ... his passport."

"But after October thirteen not a penny was withdrawn from Manefeldt's accounts. You said so yourself."

DeKok stared at the old make-up case and the heap of rags.

"They never executed their plan." It sounded somber. "Something went wrong. Somebody killed the Baron and Jantje Brewer hanged himself in despair."

"Was he guilty?

DeKok refused to look at him, there was a dissatisfied look on his face as he answered.

"What's guilt? The plan, the entire stunt was probably figured out by Jack. That's why he felt responsible. Jack Stuff liked the Baron very much. Called him his friend ... a gentleman ... the only one he had ever met. And exactly *this* man is killed, probably because of Jack's machinations. The realization became an obsession during the lonely hours in the cell." The gray sleuth sighed deeply. "Jantje saw only one way to expiate his guilt. He sacrificed his own life. A few days ago you asked me about an argument for the defense. I told you then that I would give it when I found the real killer. Well ... for the time being this is my plea on behalf of Johan Brewer."

"And what about the murderer?"

"I'll get him," DeKok answered grimly. "I swear it."

He cast a last glance at the old suitcase and its contents, ambled over to the coat rack and grabbed his raincoat.

"Where are you going?" asked Vledder.

"I'm going to see Lowee. It's been too long since my last cognac."

"I should have known," murmured Vledder.

* * *

The small barkeeper smiled.

"Was I right or was I right?"

DeKok lifted the big balloon glass and sipped from his cognac before he answered.

"The Baron," he said tiredly, "*was* an over-the-hill actor."

Lowee's friendly, mousey face gleamed with pride.

"I *knows* it," he chirped. "The Baron were an *arteest*! He did them movements of Oliver and he done looked like the guy that played Cyranac."

"Oliver? Oliver Hardy?"

"Nah . . . the other, the skinny one, the Hamlet guy."

"Lawrence Olivier"

"As I said . . . Oliver."

"And the other, Cyranac?"

"Don't know his moniker. Played the guy with the schnazz, a Yank I thinks."

DeKok realized that Lowee meant the distinguished American actor Jose Ferrer, who played Cyrano de Bergerac, but he let it slide.

"Yes," said DeKok, "I know who you mean. But the Baron performed according to a text by Johan Brewer."

Lowee looked puzzled.

"Johan Brewer?"

126

"Sure, you know him," said DeKok nonchalantly and sipped from his cognac.

Lowee's face fell, he felt attacked in his theatrical knowledge.

"Jack Stuff," clarified DeKok, "you know him as Jack Stuff. His real name is Johan Brewer and he wrote the role the Baron was supposed to play." DeKok waited a second, looked at the barkeeper and then added: "The role of a Blaricum millionaire."

Lowee avoided his gaze, wiped a hand on his apron, busied himself with a glass.

"I . . . I knows nuthin about that." It sounded unconvincing.

DeKok shrugged his shoulders.

"Jack Stuff is dead and the Baron is dead. I mean, there is no reason not to be open with me."

Little Lowee lifted the bottle.

"Another one?" he asked cheerfully. It was a transparent attempt to change the subject. DeKok took hold of the arm with the bottle.

"There is no reason at all, not to be open with me," he insisted.

Lowee freed his arm with a gentle tug and poured.

"I tole you . . . I knows nuthin about it."

"But they used to come here . . . together."

"Who?"

"Jack Stuff and the Baron."

"Well, yeah, they usta have a beer, now and then."

"And they used to talk?"

"I guess so."

DeKok's friendly face changed. Lowee's reluctant attitude irritated him.

"I never knew," he said sharply, "that you were in the habit of protecting murderers."

The slender barkeeper looked shocked.

"Tha's a lie . . . tha's a rotten thing to say."

127

DeKok shifted his weight on the barstool and gave Lowee a penetrating look.

"Listen, Lowee," he said patiently. "You and me ... we knew Jack Stuff. He's been selling and trading for years. But above all, he was a schemer, a planner. A smart guy with ideas, but always just a little unlucky with failure after failure. You know what I mean ... always just a little too late, a little short, or a little less thorough. Just bad luck ..." He stopped. His face assumed a melancholy expression. "I didn't want him dead, Lowee. I didn't want him to die the way he did ... lonely and alone in a cell with a strip of his own shirt around his neck. You don't wish that on anybody." He leaned forward and tapped the small barkeeper on the chest. "And you know what, Lowee. Deep inside that *gnaws* at me ... because I was the guy who locked him up." He paused again, rubbed his face with a tired gesture. "I'm not all that good when it comes to making speeches," he went on, "that's not my style. And far be it from me to convert you to the side of justice. It would be wasted time anyway." He raised a threatening finger in the air. "But take it from me, Lowee, If I ever discover that you could have helped me to find the Baron's murderer ..."

He did not complete the sentence, gave the barkeeper one last, long, hard look and slid off his barstool. Slowly he walked toward the exit.

A silence fell over the small, intimate little bar of Little Lowee and the barkeeper watched with mixed emotions as DeKok went out the door.

Vledder, too, came off his stool. He had listened with amazement to the outburst of his old mentor. He could not figure out the basis for the threat. Why should Lowee know anything? With a thoughtful look on his face he followed DeKok. At the door he looked around. Lowee looked crestfallen, the bottle still in his hand. The snifter with DeKok's second drink stood on the counter ... untouched.

10

They walked along the Rear Fort Canal. A drizzly rain came steadily down. The elms along the canal dripped and the cobblestones gleamed in the sparse light of the lampposts. The girls in their scanty clothes shivered in door openings ... idle. There was little interest in the delights of the Quarter. The weather had put a damper on the ardor of the clients.

DeKok pulled up the collar of his raincoat and pushed his hat further down over his forehead. He felt as miserable as the weather and his feet hurt.

Deep creases crept across his forehead. He had the confusing feeling that he *knew* the solution to the murder ... he *almost* knew how things fit together. But the final link remained elusive, just beyond his grasp. Somewhere, buried deep in his subconscious, was hidden the clue he lacked. He racked his brains, let all aspects of the case pass in review, but he could not make the connection. The missing link could not be identified.

Vledder walked next to him. They had not exchanged a word since they had left the bar. The young Inspector glanced aside and studied the familiar face.

"I didn't think you were very nice to Lowee," he began carefully.

"I wasn't," agreed DeKok.

"Are you sure he knows something?"

129

"I don't think he knows a thing about it."

"B-but . . ." Vledder stuttered with surprise, ". . . but . . . then why?"

"Lowee is a creature of the underworld," answered DeKok, licking raindrops off his lips. "I know him, have known him for a long time. I know how he reacts. I was just speculating on his feeling of comradeship, his sentimentality and . . . eh, and the fact that he likes me." He turned suddenly and faced Vledder, his face was red and his tone changed to one of anger. "Darn it," he exclaimed, "do you think I *enjoyed* playing that game. It was low, real low."

Shocked, Vledder did not respond.

They passed a series of "leaning" houses. The houses in this part of town actually lean forward. Because the houses are narrow and stairs are steep, hoisting is the only way to get big items inside. Large objects are hoisted by means of hooks from the attic windows. The houses are built on a slant to avoid damaging the furniture against the facade as it is hoisted to the desired floor. From Old Acquaintance Alley they took the bridge toward Old Church Square with small houses built between the buttresses of the ancient church. They walked through the Anna Cross Street. Sheltered by the leaning facade of one of the houses, they saw a prostitute. She looked attractive and appetizing in the half-light of the narrow street. She was short and pleasantly rounded. Firm legs reached from below a ridiculously short plastic raincoat to shoes with very high heels. The gray sleuth stopped when he saw her and lifted his hat in a polite greeting. She looked at him, recognition in her eyes.

"DeKok . . . with kay-oh-kay," she giggled. "I haven't seen you for some time."

"I didn't need you for anything," smiled DeKok.

"Just as well."

"But I've always been nice to you," grinned DeKok.

She wrinkled her nose.

"Except that one time when I rolled that guy for two hundred."

"That was stupid." DeKok shrugged his shoulders. He placed a hand on her round shoulder. "Do you know Jack is dead?"

"I heard about it," she said, lowering her head.

"Didn't you and he have a thing for each other?"

"That was a long time ago."

"Ah, but old flames never die. Have you seen him since?"

"Sometimes."

"When was the last time?"

She looked up and down the street, placed a foot against the wall behind her and leaned back. Vledder suddenly saw that she wore no panties. Blushing, he turned his gaze away.

"Last week," she said, unaware she was exposing herself.

"That was shortly before he died."

She bit her lip.

"He came by, one evening. 'Do you still love me, my girl?' he asked." She made a sad gesture. "He always asked that when he saw me."

"And?"

"So I said: 'Sure, boy, how much is it worth to you?' . . . I always answered the same." Her bright red nails plucked at the hem of her raincoat. Absent-mindedly she closed the front of the coat, more or less covering herself. "As if I would have ever charged him. I would never asked Jack for money. We're old friends, you see."

"*Per amore*," nodded DeKok.

"What's that?"

"For love."

"Love," she said contemptuously, "who believes in *that*?"

"Me . . . and Jack Stuff."

"Jack," she snorted, "was a dear boy, but he lived on a merry-go-round and never knew he had to pay for every ride."

"And you?"

131

"What?"

"Do you know?"

"Damn right," she sighed. "Nothing is free in this world and that's what I told him too."

"When?"

"That night."

"Why?"

She sadly shook her head.

"Oh, he was on cloud nine again. 'Girl,' he said, 'in a few days I'm coming to get you. Then it'll be over with the business. No more putting out.' And I said: 'Oh, yes, and what'll we eat?' Then he started to laugh. 'From the dough,' he said, 'great big wads of dough.' He sounded like he meant it."

"And," urged DeKok gently, "how did he propose to lay his hands on that kind of money?"

"I don't know." She shrugged her shoulders.

"Didn't he say *anything*?"

"Oh, yes. He was very excited. No problems, done deal and all that. The plans were ready and they only had to pick up the money."

"They?"

"Jack and the Baron. They were in it together. And then there was a Belgian."

"A Belgian?" DeKok looked surprised.

"A young Belgian," she grinned, "from Antwerp. A little sneak, according to Jack. At first the Baron didn't want him to be part of it. He didn't like the Belgian. But Jack convinced him in the end. They needed him."

"What for?"

Again she shrugged her shoulders, causing the front of her coat to fall open once more. She brought her foot down and leaned her back against the wall. The coat closed. She crossed her arms below her breasts. There was rejection in her attitude.

132

"I don't know," she said, irked. "I didn't listen all that close, you know. Jack was always full of ideas, always had plans. After a while you just tuned it out."

"Think hard, Marie," urged DeKok, a compelling tone in his voice. "Why did they need the Belgian?"

She lowered her head, thinking. Suddenly she looked up, her face lit up with a pleased smile.

"Papers," she said triumphantly. "That was *it*. The Belgian had papers."

* * *

"What sort of papers?"

DeKok pushed his chair back and placed his legs on the desk.

"Manefeldt's papers."

"Uncle Archibald?"

"Yes," nodded DeKok. "No matter how much the Baron looked like the millionaire, when push came to shove, he had to be able to *prove* he was who he said he was, i.e. Archibald Manefeldt from Blaricum, a man with an extremely advantageous bank account. Without proper identification the entire masquerade would be a fiasco. The Baron would have to face people who *knew* Manefeldt."

"So, who's the Belgian?"

"Think, my boy," grinned DeKok. "Put your imagination to work," he said cheerfully. "Who is the 'third man'? Who is the most likely suspect for that role?"

Vledder looked perplexed when he realized what DeKok was suggesting.

"Raymond Verbruggen!"

"Excellent," said DeKok, "really excellent. Raymond Verbruggen, the Belgian gentleman, as Maria Noyes described him."

"The man with the green DS21," sighed Vledder and thought about the coincidence. Only in Amsterdam could one meet an almost naked girl in the street and casually pick up an important clue in a murder case.

DeKok pulled his lower lip and let it plop back. His face was pensive.

"Verbruggen," he said after a while, "is clearly the man in the background. I think he was the one who provided Manefeldt's picture. He was the only one able to do so."

"The picture in the make-up case?"

"Exactly. Verbruggen has exploited his relationship with Abigail and her mother in order to milk them for information about Archibald Manefeldt."

"Let's arrest him," proposed Vledder eagerly.

DeKok looked at him and shook his head.

"You've suggested that before," he replied testily. "Why? The same question will have to be posed . . . on what grounds?"

"Murder."

"Murder of who?"

"The Baron. He's the only one of the three conspirators who's still alive."

"And that is proof?" DeKok grinned. "And what about motive? Did he have anything to gain by the Baron's death? On the contrary, if we have analyzed the plan correctly, the death of Ferdinand Ferkades also meant the death of *his* dreams. The Baron was the only one able to impersonate the millionaire. Without him, the plan was busted. It would be difficult, well nigh impossible, to find another actor capable of playing the role . . . besides, the time factor would be an impediment. No," emphasized DeKok, shaking his head, ". . . for the time being there's no reason to rob our Belgian friend of his freedom."

"But Verbruggen delivered the papers. Clearly he's an accomplice," objected Vledder.

DeKok spread wide his arms.

"An accomplice to what? Fraud? Nothing has happened yet, not even an attempt. There were plans and preparations, but no intent within the meaning of the Law." He paused. "And as far as that green car is concerned . . . Verbruggen's car has never been in an accident."

"How do you know that?" Vledder was stunned.

"I asked a friend in Traffic Control to pull him over for a routine safety check. They pretended that one of his brake lights wasn't working. Dr. Eskes was kind enough to have a technician on the scene to take some paint samples. Verbruggen never had an inkling."

Vledder looked at him with admiration.

"But of course, you had the paint compared to the slivers found at the scene of Martha's accident . . . and the comparison was negative?"

DeKok nodded, a bit smugly.

"You *do* think of everything," concluded Vledder.

"I try to," said DeKok and grimaced. "I don't always succeed, but I try."

The phone rang. For once DeKok was closer than Vledder and he lifted the receiver.

"DeKok . . ."

He replaced the receiver without another word.

"Something the matter?" questioned Vledder.

"The Commissaris," grinned DeKok, ". . . he wants to see me."

* * *

The commissarial office was blue with smoke. It irritated DeKok's eyes and he closed them in an attempt to wash away the stinging of the acrid cigar smoke. Through the clouds of smoke he saw the Commissaris behind his desk and he discovered Chief-Inspector Everhard, the chief of Narcotics in an easy chair near the window.

Across from him was Inspector Stekel. The Commissaris and Stekel were smoking the large cigars the Commissaris always kept in a box on his desk.

DeKok coughed demonstratively, wrinkled his nose and snorted.

"You must have confiscated a lot of hash, lately," he said sarcastically, "You can cut the air in here with a knife."

"Pure English Melange," answered Everhard unperturbed, pointing at his ever-present pipe.

The old Inspector had never liked the Chief of Narcotics, they had had a number of run-ins in the past, violent differences of opinion.

As the Commissaris moved from behind his desk, he waved toward an easy chair around the seating arrangement. When DeKok sat down, the Commissaris courteously extinguished his cigar and threw the cold stub in a trash can. He put the trash can in the hall outside. The Commissaris would not allow cold cigar stubs in the room. Although aware that DeKok had stopped smoking more than ten tears ago, before it became fashionable to do so, the two Narcotics people continued to puff away.

"We have to talk, DeKok," said the Commissaris as he took the remaining seat around the low table. "It is important. Perhaps it will affect your investigation as well. Everhard and Stekel have approached me to . . . eh, to coordinate." He paused and placed the tips of his long, pale fingers against each other, forming a little steeple with his hands. From across his finger tips he looked at DeKok. "Perhaps," he added, "I should say that these gentlemen have come to complain about you."

"Complain about me?" DeKok was genuinely surprised.

"Yes." The Commissaris spoke formally, "Both gentlemen are of the opinion that you are hampering their own investigations."

"Ridiculous." DeKok grinned foolishly. "What investigations?"

Everhard pushed forward to the edge of his chair.

"You allowed Jack Stuff to die, practically right under your nose . . . without giving us the opportunity to talk to him. Who knows what he could have told us about his relationships among the addicts and their dealers."

"Jantje committed suicide," said DeKok evenly ". . . and he didn't ask for help from anybody. I would also like to point out that your division has interrogated Johan Brewer at least twice during the last six months." He took a deep breath. "That means one of two things: either Jantje had nothing to say, or the interrogations were inept."

Everhard slammed his pipe into the ashtray, breaking the stem. His face was red with anger.

"I categorically forbid you," he said vehemently, "to criticize the people in my department."

The Commissaris intervened soothingly.

"Of course DeKok cannot be blamed for the death of Johan Brewer," he said stiffly. "It's absurd to suggest it. Also, I distinctly recall that your department was informed immediately after Brewer's arrest, in connection with the hashish that was found on him. Again *my* Inspector cannot be blamed." Briefly DeKok recognized the competent police officer the Commissaris had been in the past, before he became an accomplished interdepartmental politician waiting for his pension. "It seems to me," continued the Commissaris, "that it would be more fruitful if we put recriminations regarding Brewer behind us and concentrated on Count's Gate. Surely, that is more important."

"Count's Gate?" asked DeKok, again surprised.

The Commissaris gave him a meaningful look.

"Number 37 . . . well known to you." He gestured in the direction of Everhard and Stekel. "The gentlemen are convinced," he went on, "that Abigail Manefeldt's 'Beauty Salon' has nothing to do with the proclaimed purposes of such an establishment. They feel strongly that it is but a . . . eh, a *front* for an extensive drug operation. People who enter under the guise of needing various beauty treatments, are provided with the drug of their choice . . . most certainly the choices includes hashish, morphine, opium and heroin. Obviously in exchange for stiff prices. Smaller dealers are provided with crack-cocaine and amphetamines and such like. Isn't that so . . . eh?"

Everhard nodded agreement.

"It's a sophisticated distribution center, to say the least . . . well camouflaged. The big wheel behind it all is . . ."

". . . Raymond Verbruggen," completed DeKok.

"Raymond Verbruggen," repeated Everhard with a deep sigh. "We've had Count's Gate under surveillance for some time, but since you and Vledder have visited there several times . . ." He waved in the direction of his colleague. "Stekel has seen you himself and since then the operation seems to have been stopped. There's no activity. Visitors are sent away." He paused. "We had hoped that it would be a temporary cessation of activities. But since you had his car checked . . ." He did not complete the sentence.

DeKok rubbed his face.

"I understand," he said hoarsely. "It was just one coincidence too many and Verbruggen became doubly alert." He shook his head and looked at Everhard. "But surely you don't think that if I had known . . ."

The Narcotics Chief smiled reluctantly.

"Of course not. We're to blame as well. Perhaps we should have informed you, at least your Commissaris. But you understand, we wanted to keep it under cover as much as possible."

DeKok stared into the distance, blinking his eyes at the smoke.

"How did you get all that information about Abigail, Count's Gate and Raymond Verbruggen?"

Everhard looked at him searchingly.

"Why do you want to know?"

"I'm interested. "DeKok shrugged his shoulders. "I'm just interested because of a possible connection with my own case."

The Chief Inspector reached down next to his chair and produced a briefcase.

"An anonymous tip," he confessed honestly. "In writing." He handed DeKok a folded piece of paper.

DeKok looked at it intently. It turned out to be a paper napkin, yellow, a bit wrinkled. All sorts of information about drug deliveries, complete with times and dates, was scribbled in a spidery handwriting. Raymond Verbruggen and Count's Gate were named specifically.

DeKok read the note several times, absorbing every word. Then he unfolded the napkin completely and held it up against the light. In several places there were reddish-brown, somewhat greasy spots. Everhard watched his reactions tensely.

"And?" he asked curiously.

DeKok handed him back the napkin.

"Greasepaint," he said enigmatically, "just stage make-up."

11

Inspector DeKok paced up and down the large detective room at the ancient police station in Warmoes Street. It was one of his habits and it helped him think. His thoughts seemed to arrange themselves in more orderly fashion to the cadence of his steps. There was no denying that the new developments had taken him aback. He reflected that in police circles as well, the left hand often did not know what the right hand was doing. The thought had plagued him frequently. At least the speculation of whether or not a tip about Verbruggen had reached Narcotics was now at an end. But it remained strange, it simply did not fit into the pattern that he had imagined. He had been less surprised to learn that the fashionable house at Count's Gate did not contain a Beauty Salon. Aunt Aleida's bizarre make-up was scarcely an endorsement for the professionalism of her daughter. A veritable regiment of questions seemed to confront him. Did Raymond Verbruggen obtain the drugs in Antwerp? Did Aunt Aleida know about his activities? How did that fit in with the killing of Martha Noyes? Martha? Suddenly he stopped, causing another detective to bump into him, spilling a folder full of papers on the floor. DeKok paid no attention.

"Robert!" he shouted. "Robert Antoine Dijk!" His deep voice echoed against the walls, overpowering all the other noises in the large room.

The young Inspector's head popped up from behind a row of file cabinets. A moment later he emerged in full view. DeKok smirked indulgently.

"As usual, you look like a picture, Robert Antoine," said DeKok mockingly. "Such a *interesting* color. Heliotrope is it?"

The young Inspector smiled politely. He was known for his fashionable clothes and knew that DeKok liked to make jokes about it. As a matter of fact, his suit was a sedate beige, with just a hint of reddish-pink in the material. Dijk was one of the Inspectors DeKok liked to call on first, if he needed additional help. The younger Inspectors were always glad to help out the old man and not a few of them were secretly jealous of Vledder's close working relationship with the legendary sleuth.

None of that entered into DeKok's mind as he pointed at the old, battered make-up case.

"Please take that to the lab and give Dr. Eskes one of the sticks of reddish-brown greasepaint. Ask him if it's possible to compare it with the spots on the napkin."

"What napkin?"

"He has that already," explained DeKok. "Chief-Inspector Everhard of Narcotics was to deliver it personally."

"And the case?"

"You take that, complete with the wrappings, to Mrs. Louise Graaf. Vledder will give you the address. If she recognizes the case as belonging to Ferdinand Ferkades, she may keep it . . . under *one* condition. She has to give you one of the letters of her ex-husband."

"If she has them."

"She'll have them," said DeKok with quiet conviction. "Don't worry about that. I'm sure she kept all his love letters. But make it clear to her that we're *not* interested in the contents. That will remain secret. We're concerned with the handwriting, the handwriting of Ferdinand Ferkades."

"And when I have the letter?"

"Then you go back to Dr. Eskes and ask him to have someone compare the handwriting in the letter with that on the napkin."

Dijk nodded understanding of the instructions. He took the address that Vledder had written on a piece of paper and hoisted the make-up case under one arm.

"And have Dr. Eskes call me also, if there's *no* match between the handwriting," DeKok called after him.

"And what are you going to do?" asked Vledder.

"What are *we* going to do," corrected DeKok.

"All right, what are *we* going to do?"

"We're going to Blaricum ... we're going to ask Nephew Archibald if he's ever owned a green car."

"What!?"

"Did I speak Russian again?" asked DeKok with well-feigned amazement.

* * *

"You want to park near the church again?"

"No, this time we'll drive straight into the driveway." He grinned boyishly. "If you want, you may even turn on the siren."

Vledder turned off to Blaricum.

"Not too smart," he commented disapprovingly. "If young Archibald has something on his conscience, he'll take off like a scared rabbit."

"They all have a bad conscience."

"All of them?"

"Murder," said DeKok in a sepulchral voice, "is the beginning ... never the end."

"Whatever *do* you mean?"

"People are driven to murder," DeKok said slowly, "because they see the death of a fellow human being as the only solution to their problems. Only *after* the deed do they discover that they have created a whole new set of problems ... more serious and more irrevocable than the problems that led to the killing." He smiled sadly. "Perhaps that's the tragedy of a murderer . . . the tragedy of every crime."

Vledder made an impatient gesture without taking his eyes off the road.

"How does that apply to *this* situation?"

"Aunt Helen . . . her eccentric husband was definitely a problem for her. And then there was Martha . . ."

"Martha had a problem?" interrupted Vledder.

"Her invalid sister."

"But there's nothing to show that it oppressed her overly much," protested Vledder.

DeKok pushed his lower lip forward.

"What did you think of the nursing home where we saw Maria Noyes?"

"Nice, luxurious."

"Exactly my impression: nice and luxurious." He turned toward Vledder. "Care to make a guess what it would cost to stay there, for instance *until it pleases Our Dear Lord to take you away*?"

"A small fortune."

"Eight days before her death," DeKok said softly, "Martha Noyes deposited seventy five percent of the amount necessary in escrow with an attorney who has since been appointed as executor of her estate."

Vledder swallowed.

"But . . . but that could not have been money from the farm," he said superfluously.

"Right. That wasn't sold until months after her death . . . at a fire-sale price, as you expressed it." He paused and watched Vledder as he turned into Sheep's Lane. "I also talked to the family doctor, Doctor Keypers, a friendly, understanding man who had a lot of contact with both sisters. Did you know that Martha was seriously ill?"

144

"Ill?"

"Cancer," sighed DeKok. "Dr. Keypers estimated she had less than six months left to live."

"And she knew that?"

DeKok scratched the tip of his nose.

"She knew that."

* * *

The gravel crunched underneath the tires. Vledder switched off the engine and put the keys in his pocket. DeKok prepared himself to get out of the car, but made no move to actually do so.

"Should I open the door for sir?" asked Vledder with a grin.

"I'm waiting until someone comes out to greet us," said DeKok evenly, staring through the windshield.

"In that case we may have a long wait," joked Vledder. "Surely you don't think that Archibald is waiting for us with the welcome mat out?"

"Who knows," answered DeKok, glancing up at the house. "Why don't you blow the horn a few times?"

Vledder complied. Three, four times the braying sound of the car-horn echoed against the house. A few sparrows flew up and a rabbit hopped across the driveway. There was no other reaction to the sound. DeKok opened the car door and stepped out.

"Mr. Vanderwehr is not at home," he concluded laconically.

Leisurely he strolled toward the front door. The spider webs still decorated the top part of the door. Passing the closed shutters, he walked toward the back of the house and found the kitchen door locked. With a feeling of having seen it all before, he produced Handy Henkie's little instrument and unlocked the door in a few seconds. The hinges screeched and DeKok waited until the noise had died away. Then he stepped inside, followed by Vledder.

The kitchen presented the same desolate picture as before. The corridor and the room had not changed either. The clock still pointed to twelve o'clock. Only the clammy smell of dampness and dust seemed to have intensified, as if the rotting process had been speeded up. DeKok shivered involuntarily and Vledder darted anxious eyes around. There was something threatening, something undefinable evil about the neglected house.

"You want me to look upstairs?" asked Vledder in a whisper.

"I'll come with you," said DeKok.

One behind the other they ascended the wide staircase and looked into the rooms on the second floor. There was nobody. The rooms had not been entered for some time. The dust covered everything in deep, undisturbed layers. By means of a narrower staircase they reached the attic floor. Underneath an open skylight they found a blue camp stove with a butane tank. Cans of food were scattered around and a few feet away, near where the roof met the floor of the attic, they saw an old mattress and a number of blankets.

"He's gone," said Vledder solemnly.

DeKok did not bother to answer. He bent over near a china plate, took the spoon from the plate and looked at the bottom of the spoon. Then he directed his attention to the mattress. Under the dirty pillowcase he found a hypodermic. It was a large, old fashioned hypodermic, made of glass and chrome steel. A broken needle protruded from one end.

"The murder weapon?" ventured Vledder, eyeing the discarded instrument.

DeKok lifted the hypodermic carefully by the stump of the broken needle and held it up to the light. The inside of the cylinder was covered with a dirty brown substance, like the tar deposits from a tobacco pipe. He turned toward Vledder.

"Do you have any plastic bags on you? Evidence bags?"

"Of course," answered Vledder, producing a small packet of strong plastic bags from an inside pocket. "There's more in the car," he added.

146

DeKok dropped the hypodermic in the bag Vledder held open for him. Vledder sealed the bag while DeKok pointed at the spoon he had lifted earlier.

"I want that to go to the lab as well," said DeKok.

"The plate, or the spoon . . . or both?"

"Just the spoon, I want to know if it's been used to dissolve drugs."

"I don't see a candle," observed Vledder.

"You can also hold the spoon over a camp stove."

DeKok picked up an empty can, looked at it, smelled it and replaced it next to the stove. In a corner of the attic he found an old medicine cabinet. There were a number of empty ampules inside.

"You think he might come back?" asked Vledder.

"Don't know. I have the feeling he's already been gone for a few days. Some of the food remnants have mold on them."

With the spoon, the hypodermic and the empty ampules in plastic bags they climbed down from the attic. Downstairs, in the corridor, DeKok stood still. A strange, inexplicable chill came over him. Again he shivered. He pressed his lips together and looked around, looking for an explanation, but unable to find it. The feeling teased his nerves.

"I won't leave here," he hissed between his teeth, "until I've found him."

"What . . . found who?"

DeKok did not answer. He went into the kitchen and stopped in front of the old coal stove. The oven doors were still hanging precariously from bent hinges and the cooking surface was still a rusty mess. He turned around. Slowly his gaze traveled among the disorder in the filthy kitchen. Suddenly he looked at Vledder.

"Where's the cellar?" he asked.

"Is there a cellar?" asked Vledder, puzzled.

"There has to be," nodded DeKok, ". . . there has to be a place to store coal."

"Maybe there's a shed outside?"

DeKok walked into the garden. A strange unrest possessed him. Carefully he walked around, every sinew under tension. His sharp gaze did not miss a single detail and he continually compared what he saw with the picture in his mind from the previous visit. The green was darker, some bushes had bloomed and some had dropped their blossoms. But he ignored the strictly natural manifestations. Suddenly he stopped, like a retriever "pointing". His right arm came horizontal, an outstretched finger at the end of his hand.

"The terrace," he panted, "the terrace."

"What's the matter with the terrace?"

"The grass is gone from between the tiles."

* * *

They watched with expressionless faces as two workmen shoveled away the earth from beneath the tiles. The tiles were stacked in a heap to one side, forming a bizarre, surrealistic shadow in the light of the waning sun from behind the trees. As it got darker, the headlights from a police van and some auxiliary lighting provided by the local constabulary helped to illuminate the area. Dr. Rusteloos, summoned from Amsterdam, stood with one foot in the sand and directed the workmen. When a shod foot became visible, he told them to stop. The photographer hovered near and started taking pictures. Dr. Rusteloos, hands protected by rubber gloves, carefully removed some excess dirt from around the foot and then tugged on the trouser leg that became visible. With a few tugs and pulls he unearthed a leg. He looked up at DeKok.

"How long has he been here?"

"I estimate about ten days," said DeKok. He shrugged his shoulders. "But he's been dead for at least six months."

"You know who it is?"

"Archibald Manefeldt."

Dr. Rusteloos was surprised.

148

"Didn't I do an autopsy on him, not too long ago?"

"That was the wrong man," said DeKok curtly.

"The wrong man?"

"Yes, an over-the-hill actor."

"Well, I couldn't see that from the outside," smiled the police pathologist. "Or from the inside," he joked.

DeKok hid his amusement behind an even face and pointed at the newly visible leg.

"I'd like to know how he died."

"We'll see," sighed the doctor. He gestured toward the workmen. Carefully they dug around the corpse. When the head became visible, a murmur went round the onlookers. The head seemed larger than normal. Upon further investigation they found a plastic bag, tied tightly around the neck of the corpse, shutting off all air.

"You want to remove it here?" asked DeKok, pointing at the plastic bag.

"No," answered the pathologist. "I want him on the table as he is now." He glanced at his watch. "It's late anyway," he continued, "I might as well get started as soon as possible."

DeKok nodded grateful agreement.

They put the corpse into a body bag and on a stretcher and shoved it into the police van for transportation to the local hospital. Dr. Rusteloos was to avail himself of the Blaricum facilities.

DeKok lingered for a moment, looked at the hole in the ground, the freakish stack of tiles and shivered for the third time that day.

* * *

"A bashed-in skull?"

"More than likely with a single blow," said Vledder. "Diagonally from behind. Dr. Rusteloos suggested a heavy, round object, a table leg, a large vase, a statuette, or something like that."

149

"Was he recognizable?"

Vledder wiped his mouth with the back of his hand, recalling the sight of the dead man.

"He was," he began hesitatingly, "about fifty-five, sixty years old. Dr. Rusteloos agreed with that. He was very similar in height and looks to the man we found at the church wall. But he was better dressed. The face had been ravaged by time, but the big, droopy moustache was unmistakable." He took a deep breath. "I don't think there's any question about it. The corpse from beneath the tiles is that of Archibald Manefeldt."

DeKok stood up and walked over to the coffeepot. He came back with two big mugs of coffee. He placed one in front of Vledder.

"Fresh," he said, "just made it."

"Thanks," said Vledder, "I needed that. It wasn't exactly a picnic, this time."

DeKok smiled.

"I was glad you volunteered to attend the autopsy. I really didn't feel like it myself."

Vledder sipped his coffee and DeKok slurped his, comfortably and totally unabashed. Coffee was one of his weaknesses and he always slurped it. Vledder had wondered about that in the past, had speculated that it might have something to do with DeKok's early life as the son of a fisherman. But he had stopped noticing it, other than in a completely positive way. There was something infinitely comforting about watching DeKok slurp his coffee with such obvious pleasure and in complete relaxation. Over the years it has changed from a rude, unpleasant sound to a familiar, friendly noise.

"How did you know Manefeldt was buried there?" asked Vledder.

"I didn't know. I was simply convinced that he was no longer alive. There were too many indications that he was dead."

"Such as?"

DeKok stared into the distance and slurped his coffee. The two were isolated in a corner of the large room, there were at least three empty desks between them and the nearest of the other occupants of the room. DeKok had obtained his desk at the far end of the room, close to the windows, by seniority and perseverance. Naturally Vledder's desk had been placed next to his when they started to work together regularly.

"Manefeldt," began DeKok, "would usually leave in the spring to go roaming and would return in the fall. Contrary to his usual habits, we were expected to believe that he *left* in the fall, this time. Of course, the possibility was not excluded, but . . . he also withdrew no money after October thirteen. That leaves the question of what he used to live on. Further investigation of his bank records revealed that, despite the odd jobs he used to take on, he also regularly withdrew funds during his trips. Nephew Archibald tried to reach his uncle after the death of Aunt Helen. He placed advertisements in most of the major European papers and had announcements made on radio and via the Automobile Club. Manefeldt did not respond. He was not at the funeral of Aunt Helen."

"But that doesn't explain how his corpse wound up underneath the tiles of the terrace."

"No, it doesn't. But he's been there only a short time. Ten days ago there was still grass between the tiles."

"But he's been dead for more than six months."

"First the body was stashed elsewhere."

"Obviously. But where?"

"I think he must have been hidden, or buried, somewhere in the immediate vicinity of the estate." He paused, looked into his empty mug and placed it on the desk. "Look . . . it's almost certain that Manefeldt was killed between October thirteen, the day he withdrew money from his bank, and November three, the day Aunt Helen died. Where was he at that time?"

"Home."

"Exactly, at his house in Blaricum."

"But, in that case, Aunt Helen *knew* what had happened," said Vledder, wide-eyed.

"That's exactly right," asserted DeKok with emphasis. "And it affected her health to such a degree that it made her ill and she died. At the very least it must have hastened her death." He paused, glanced at his empty mug, but manfully carried on. "I can well imagine that. Alone ... with your conscience in that desolate house, knowing that somewhere near is the corpse of your murdered husband. You have to have strong nerves to withstand that. I don't mind telling you that this afternoon the shivers ran up and down my spine." He shrugged his shoulders, smiled foolishly. "I think it's a strange, sinister house. I had the feeling that Manefeldt's ghost was still on the prowl."

Thoughtfully Vledder picked up DeKok's empty mug and his own. A little later he returned with two full mugs and placed the one with a lot of sugar in front of DeKok. DeKok cupped his hands around the mug as if to warm them and took a greedy slurp. Vledder reseated himself at his own desk.

"You know," said the young Inspector, "I was suddenly reminded about what Maria Noyes told us in the nursing home. I mean what she said *Martha* has said about Aunt Helen."

DeKok rubbed his face with a flat hand.

"*The pour soul won't last much longer, she runs screaming through the house,*" quoted DeKok. "*She suffered from nightmares. She almost never slept. She saw ghosts everywhere.*"

Vledder nodded, taking in stride DeKok's ability to quote verbatim a conversation he had heard only once.

"And then," amplified Vledder, "Aunt Helen's visit to the two sisters in the middle of the night ..."

DeKok raked his fingers through his hair.

"Then is when she must have told Martha."

"What?"

"About the murder."

"Martha knew who had killed Manefeldt?"

DeKok nodded slowly.

"The knowledge killed her."

12

It was already past noon when DeKok finally made his appearance at the office. A good night's rest had restored his spirit and his good humor. He laughed cheerfully at the Watch Commander and took the stairs with the vitality of a much younger man. One of his colleagues accosted him in the corridor, leading to the detective room.

"The Commissaris has asked for you several times."

"Aha, and how did he sound?"

"Normal . . . same as always."

"I was afraid of that," answered DeKok somberly.

Before his colleague could react, DeKok had bounded away toward the end of the long corridor and entered the office at the end.

The stately police chief looked disturbed as DeKok came in.

"Oh . . . sit down, DeKok," said the Chief, quickly recovering his formal good manners. "I heard that you've dug up a *second* Manefeldt."

"The first," corrected DeKok. "The other man wasn't Manefeldt."

The Commissaris waved away any objections.

"Certainly, certainly . . . but you *thought* it was Manefeldt."

Again DeKok shook his head.

155

"I never thought a thing," he said stubbornly. "The corpse at the church wall was falsely, or mistakenly identified as that of Manefeldt by his niece, Abigail and by a friendly, cooperative, but apparently myopic Mr. Verport from Utrecht."

"But who could have gained from it?"

"That," grinned DeKok, "seems to be the sort of question with which to confront Mrs. Manefeldt . . . or, as she prefers to be called, Aleida Drosselhoff, the lady you so often provide with a glass of water."

"She was my guest," blushed the Commissaris.

"So was Jack Stuff, who died downstairs in the cells," said DeKok harshly.

The Commissaris lost his temper. He suddenly sat very straight and very still in his chair.

"That . . . that was a scurrilous remark, DeKok." His voice was tense.

DeKok nodded resignedly.

"It was," he said simply, "but I won't take it back . . . and, before you send me away again, I'll leave now."

* * *

DeKok found Vledder pale and hollow-eyed, slumped behind his desk. The desk top was scattered with various pieces of paper, notes, photographs and his notebook. The screen of his computer terminal blinked insistently. DeKok gave his partner a long look.

"Something the matter?" he asked, concern in his voice. "You look as if you've seen a ghost . . . a dozen ghosts."

Vledder stretched his arms above his head and yawned.

"I didn't sleep a wink, last night."

"Why not?"

"I just couldn't sleep, couldn't get the case out of my mind."

"I see."

"So I came in early and looked through everything again, all the files, all the reports, all the information . . . right back to the moment we found the first corpse at South Church."

"And?"

Vledder cleared a space on the top of his desk and leaned his elbows on the edge. He had a discouraged look on his face.

"I can't get anywhere," he said listlessly. "At first I thought we'd be close to a solution, but that isn't so . . . that's to say, I don't see any connection." He pushed his chair back waved at the disorder on his desk.

"What you need is a cup of coffee," said DeKok, who hated to start his day without the stimulating effect of the brew. He walked over to the coffee pot and poured two mugs. He added a lot of sugar to his own and placed the other mug in front of Vledder. After Vledder had taken his first sip and DeKok had taken his first slurp, the old man looked expectantly at his colleague.

"You theorized that Manefeldt was killed between October thirteen and November three," started Vledder. "Well, all right so far . . . I can understand that much. From that it follows that he was probably at home at the time. We know that the Manefeldt's seldom received visitors. Therefore they were presumably together . . . Aunt Helen and her husband."

"You think Aunt Helen killed her husband?" DeKok's eyebrows danced briefly. For one giddy moment it seemed as if they actually exchanged places with each other. Vledder was too preoccupied to notice.

"That doesn't compute," answered Vledder, shaking his head, "if that were so, then . . . why was Martha killed? I mean, if Martha died because she knew who killed Manefeldt . . . who was *her* killer? Who could gain from her silence? Certainly not Aunt Helen . . . not any more, anyway. In the first place Aunt Helen didn't have a driver's license and didn't know how to drive and secondly . . . she had long since been dead and buried."

"Brilliant," interjected DeKok brightly, ". . . scratch off Aunt Helen."

"Wait a minute," said Vledder, "there's more. Let's assume that the couple had a visitor. A visitor who so abused the hospitality that he, or she, bashed Uncle Archibald on the head. That could make his wife an accomplice, because it raises the question: Why didn't she blow the whistle . . . why didn't she file a complaint?"

"Excellent," admired DeKok, "really excellent. And what's the answer?"

"She was either an accomplice, an active participant or . . . the visitor was dear to her, more important than the life of her eccentric husband and she became an accomplice after the fact."

"The latter," nodded DeKok. "That has to be it. Frankly, considering her age and physical condition, I find it hard to believe in Aunt Helen as an active participant. She was a 'spineless wonder', totally unequipped to withstand her tyrannical husband. We know nothing of any quarrels, or rebellion regarding his treatment of her. But that the killer was dear to her, more so because he, or she, finally did what she might have wished to do herself . . . that seems a reasonable assumption at this point. That's why she did not betray the killer. But it was a burden she was unable to carry. One night it became too much. She dressed hastily and visited Martha, her confidant."

"Yes, yes," exclaimed Vledder impatiently. "That's how far I got myself. But *who*? Who was so dear to her that she was willing to hide a murder?"

The telephone rang and DeKok lifted the receiver. After a few grunts, he replaced the instrument. Vledder looked at him tensely.

"Who was it?"

"Downstairs, the Watch Commander."

"Oh, what did he want?"

"He had a message for us . . . Archibald Vanderwehr has been taken to Wilhelmina Hospital."

"Here . . . in Amsterdam . . . why?"

"He was found unconscious with a gaping head wound."

"Where?"

"Near Count's Gate."

Vledder looked stunned as DeKok slurped the last of his coffee.

* * *

His hat in his hand, DeKok emerged from the Emergency Wing of the hospital. He had loosened his collar and tie. DeKok did not like hospitals. The atmosphere and the smell suffocated him. Vledder approached him hastily.

"And?" he ask curiously.

"In deep shock," sighed DeKok.

Vledder's face fell.

"We can't interrogate him?"

"No," DeKok shook his head dejectedly. "The outward physical condition is not too bad. A considerable wound on the forehead, above the left eye. But as I said, he's in deep shock and that's more serious. According to the doctor it will be some time before Vanderwehr will be able to speak coherently. Apparently he's been taking so much morphine lately, it's a wonder he's still alive."

"Stupid son-of-a-bitch," hissed Vledder in one of the rare instances that he forgot DeKok's dislike of strong language.

"We don't know," said DeKok, shrugging his shoulders and ignoring Vledder's lapse, "under what sort of stress Vanderwehr has been lately. Perhaps he *did* try to kill himself with an overdose . . . it could have been attempted suicide."

"Why?" Vledder grinned cynically. "The future was rosy enough for him. Just think, co-beneficiary of several millions."

159

"Forget it." DeKok shook his head. "He doesn't get a dime from the man after whom he's been named."

"Nothing?"

"No, all the millions go to niece Abigail."

"How did you find that out?"

DeKok looked sad.

"Aunt Helen and Uncle Archibald had a pre-nuptial agreement. Only the villa is in her name. I found that out while you were at the autopsy. I had called Mr. Verport to tell him he'd been mistaken. After some probing he volunteered the information about the marriage of Helena Winegarten, Aunt Helen as we know her, and Archibald Manefeldt. He also told me about the affair between Manefeldt and his sister-in-law, Aleida Drosselhoff. In some circles, he said, it was taken as an article of faith that Abigail was the result of impregnation by Archibald and Manefeldt never denied it. Eight years ago he made a Last Will and Testament in which he admitted the relationship. In case his own marriage remained childless, his entire capital was destined for Niece Abigail."

"And Vanderwehr *knew* that?"

DeKok scratched the back of his neck.

"I'm not sure ... but from a lot of circumstances ... his unchallenged stay at the villa, for instance ... I assume that all those involved are aware of the contents of the Will."

"But," swallowed Vledder, "in that case Vanderwehr has no motive to ..."

"... to kill his uncle."

"He had nothing to gain." Vledder gestured vaguely. "And at the same time, there's no motive for him to kill Martha. The two killings are connected ... one is a direct result of the other."

DeKok was thinking along different lines.

"What was Vanderwehr doing at Count's Gate?" he mused. "If that patrol car hadn't found him in time, he would have been just as dead as ..."

"Did you see him?" asked Vledder anxiously.

"Yes," DeKok answered slowly. "It *did* take some doing to get the physician to agree and it turned out to be the *only* concession he was ready to make." He smiled bitterly. "But I had to see him, I insisted. I had to be sure. This entire case has made me more careful, more suspicious. I wanted to make sure that the patient was indeed Archibald Vanderwehr."

"And?"

"Oh, it was him, no doubt about that. I recognized him at once. But he had become awfully thin, almost emaciated . . . he looked bad . . . also hadn't shaved for days."

"Did you talk to him at all?"

DeKok shook his head.

"I tried. Kept hanging around and when the nurse left the room for a moment, I did ask him a few quick questions, despite the warning." He rubbed the bridge of his nose with a little finger. "But to no avail. He didn't even seem to hear me."

"Well," said Vledder, "it seems that for the moment we're at a dead end." He bit his lip and looked pensive. "Nephew Archibald is a key figure at this point. It's just possible that questioning him may clear up the case. In any case it's certain that he . . ."

DeKok replaced his hat on top of his head and walked away, leaving Vledder in mid-sentence. Obviously he had not heard a word. Vledder followed him, a bit piqued. Just before they reached the street, DeKok turned around.

"Did you check his stuff?"

Vledder looked puzzled.

"What stuff?"

"Vanderwehr's stuff," said DeKok impatiently, "the clothes he wore when he was checked into the hospital . . . that and everything that goes with it." Without waiting for a reply, he continued his progress down the street.

Vledder stared after him, a perplexed, stupefied look on his face. There were times when he wondered if he and DeKok lived on the same planet.

* * *

Chief Inspector Everhard, the Chief of Narcotics, riffled hastily through his papers.

"My people didn't report it," he said, shaking his head. "I went through everything and there is no mention of it in their reports."

"And the house is under constant surveillance?" asked DeKok.

"Twenty four hours a day, we have a special task force assigned."

"So," said DeKok, more to himself than anybody, "if Vanderwehr had entered the house at Count's Gate, he would have been observed."

"Without a doubt . . . and it would have been reported immediately. Everything is reported."

"Where is Raymond Verbruggen now?" asked DeKok, filing away the previous information for future use.

Chief Everhard raised his hands in despair.

"Vanished from the face of the earth. The only people we've seen for some time are the old lady and the young girl."

"Aunt Aleida and Niece Abigail."

"Yes, if that's what you call them. The mother and the daughter . . . frankly, I've given some thought to terminating the operation altogether. Without Raymond Verbruggen we can't expect any action and as you well know, we have limited manpower and even less time . . . as usual."

"Where can he be?" queried DeKok, ignoring Everhard's Jeremiad. The police never had enough time and never had enough people. It was an old story and DeKok was not interested in it.

Everhard shrugged his shoulders.

"No idea. Perhaps in Belgium. We did contact the Antwerp police . . . we know that Verbruggen has relations there."

"Is that where the drugs originate?"

"It's unusual, " sighed Everhard. He hesitated, then went on. "To be honest, we have no idea about how the stuff gets into the country, or from where. We had hoped to find out by following him . . . but you ruined that for us."

"We've discussed that before," smiled DeKok. He stood up. "Are you shadowing the old lady and the girl?"

"No . . . why?"

DeKok retrieved his hat.

"Just one more question . . . would a morphine user ever use opium?"

"No," answered Everhard, "unless there was nothing else . . . in an emergency, so to speak."

DeKok nodded understanding. He swept his hat through the air in a graceful gesture reminiscent of a cavalier from times gone by and left Everhard's office. A smile danced around his lips.

* * *

They left Headquarters at Marnix Street and drove toward Elk's Canal. A light, drizzly rain clung to the windshield, augmented by the muddy splashes from other cars. It was the sort of rain that impaired vision more than a cleansing downpour, yet did not seem enough for wipers. The old VW was not equipped with a window washer. Vledder turned on the wipers and succeeded in creating some gaps between the streaks of dirt.

"What did Everhard say?"

DeKok followed the wipers with his eyes. The steady, rhythmic movement, accompanied by a regular shriek as the rubber squeezed across the almost dry windshield, tended to lull him asleep. Fragments of images flashed by his mind's eye. The peaceful corpse at the church wall ... Niece Abigail at the confrontation ... Jack Stuff in his cell ...

"What did Everhard say?" repeated Vledder.

DeKok closed his eyes, shook his head as if to clear it.

"They never saw Vanderwehr," he said absent-mindedly.

"But they should have, shouldn't they?"

DeKok rubbed his eyes.

"I don't know how they've organized the surveillance. Everhard didn't volunteer and I didn't want to ask. But I think their view may be limited. I'm almost sure they can't see *all* of Count's Gate." He peered through the windshield. "Where are we going?" he asked.

"Back to the station."

"Very good." He searched around in his pockets and Vledder expected him to produce some sort of candy. Instead his hand emerged from an inside pocket with a carefully folded handkerchief, wrapped around something. "I'll just put this in the glove compartment. Help remind me, will you?"

"What is it?" asked Vledder, darting a glance from the corner of his eyes.

"Vanderwehr's needle and some ampules."

"Morphine?"

"Yes, he had it on him when they took him to the hospital ... I confiscated it."

"What's so important about that?" asked Vledder mockingly. He shrugged his shoulders. "An - addict - has - a - needle - and - drugs." It sounded like cant.

DeKok glanced at him.

"That is so," he said simply.

* * *

Robert Antoine Dijk looked nervous and he worried with one of the buttons on the sleeve of his stylish jacket.

"Professor Eskes said that there are other cops in Amsterdam. He told me to tell you that Inspector DeKok is not the only one who needs information."

"Professor Eskes isn't telling me anything I don't know," grinned DeKok.

"He meant," explained Dijk, "that he couldn't upset the routine of his laboratory just for . . ."

DeKok waved him impatiently into silence.

"Maybe the lab should go on three shifts, then," he growled. "What about the stains on the napkin?"

"Almost certainly from the make-up case of Ferdinand Ferkades," confirmed Dijk, after consulting his notebook. DeKok thought idly that with all the aid of computers and modern storage and retrieval systems, younger detectives like Dijk and Vledder, seemed to us a lot of notebooks. DeKok had not inaugurated a new notebook for more than three years. He credited his own superior memory, blithely ignoring the fact that Vledder took most, if not all of his notes. As the thought flashed through his mind, he smiled ruefully at his own vanity.

"Excellent," he exclaimed heartily, "really excellent. What about the handwriting?"

Dijk made a helpless gesture.

"Dr. Eskes . . . eh, the Professor couldn't say much about it."

"Why not?" asked DeKok crossly. "Didn't you get a letter from Louise Graaf?"

"Sure, a whole stack . . . bound with a ribbon."

"Well, then what's the problem,?"

"Dr. Eskes, the Professor, said he didn't have time to assign it right-a-way. He lacked the personnel. He also said that he still had a hypodermic with a broken needle and a dirty old spoon. It all takes time, he said."

Dr. Eskes was one of the foremost forensic experts in the Netherlands, but he was as eccentric as he was old. DeKok had known him for a long time. Dr. Eskes had organized the fledgling forensics lab for the Amsterdam police when DeKok was still a uniformed constable.

"Well," said DeKok, rubbing his chin, "I hope he hurries... we're running out of time."

He came from behind his desk and placed a fatherly hand on Dijk's shoulder.

"Thanks, Robert, I appreciate what you did. Now I have another request."

Dijk beamed under the compliment.

"You want me to shadow somebody?" he asked eagerly. That was the thing he liked doing best. He felt he was good at it.

"Yes," nodded DeKok. "Narcotics is keeping a house under surveillance ... Count's Gate thirty-seven. I don't know exactly where they've concealed themselves, but undoubtedly within sight of the address. Now ... I want you too, to keep an eye on the place ... but from a distance. Take a car and park it near the Montelbaan Tower ... from there you can keep an eye on the entire street. Take binoculars, I don't want you to make a mistake." He placed a finger alongside his nose. Suddenly he looked like an old, crafty godfather from a gangster film. "When you see an older lady leave the house, or a young girl ... singly or together.... you let them go at first. You start following them as soon as they can no longer be observed from Count's Gate itself, you understand? I don't want Chief Inspector Everhard to think that I've set a fox among *his* chickens."

"Then what?" asked Dijk, nodding gravely.

"Nothing," said DeKok. "Nothing at all. I just want to know where they're going. No matter what you see, or hear ... you keep your distance. If it's really important, you contact us. Arrange it with the Watch Commander and," he swallowed, grinned sheepishly at himself, shook his head with a chagrined look. "... and," he added, "make sure you have a walkie-talkie, as well as the communication gear in the car."

"That's all?" asked Dijk, successfully hiding his surprise at DeKok's mention of the walkie-talkie.

DeKok nodded, a friendly, approving smile on his face.

"Take care of yourself," he said softly, concern in his voice.

Robert Antoine Dijk laughed shyly. A friendly approach always confused him. He hesitated a moment, as if wanting to say something, then he turned around and left the room. The phone rang as he closed the door behind him. Vledder picked it up.

"News?" asked DeKok, tilting his head to one side.

Vledder grinned, covering the mouthpiece with his hand.

"It's your pal, Little Lowee. He says the glasses are ready."

DeKok's face froze.

"Tell him we're on our way," he said, turning on his heel.

13

It was quiet in the poorly illuminated, intimate little bar of Little
Lowee. It was almost always quiet in the bar. If DeKok had not
known that Lowee did a brisk business late at night and had a
number of profitable sidelines, from pimping to fencing, he might
have wondered how Lowee managed to make ends meet.

There was nobody at the bar and, apart from Lowee, the only
other occupant, "Ace" Allan, was sitting at a far table, practicing
his card tricks. The slender barkeeper was behind the counter
rinsing glasses. Vledder was sure that as soon as he had rinsed all
the glasses he would start from the beginning, he was always
rinsing glasses.

Lowee placed a glass on the dripping board and hastily wiped
his hands when the two Inspectors entered. With a happy smile on
his mousy face, he reached across the bar in order to shake hands.

"Mr. DeKok," he said heartily, "I's glad to see you. Last time
you left sorta hurried like . . . too fast, really. I was *that* upset about
it."

DeKok looked serious.

"I've laid awake nights over it myself," he said.

Lowee laughed.

"Go on, you knows what I means." He took three large
snifters from the rack behind him and placed them on the bar in
front of the cops. A quick movement, and he emerged from

underneath the counter with an exclusive bottle of fine Napoleon cognac, a bottle specifically reserved for DeKok's visits. With a steady, professional movement he poured the golden liquid into the waiting glasses.

"To . . . eh, to friendship," said Lowee hesitantly, raising his glass.

DeKok smiled gently.

"To *our* friendship," he amended.

Lowee beamed and waited for DeKok to take the first sip. He watched the old sleuth over the rim of his own glass, as he joined him. Vledder moved uneasily on his high bar stool. He was too restless to enjoy a glass of cognac, no matter how fine. The ceremony irritated him and he leaned closer to the other two.

"We still don't know who killed the Baron," he said brusquely.

Little Lowee turned toward him, his friendly smile changing to an annoyed look.

"Me neither," he said evenly.

"In some circles," snorted Vledder, "the murderer is known."

Lowee's face fell.

"In them circles they knows nuthin about it," he said sharply.

DeKok intervened.

"You can't blame him," he soothed, "Vledder is impatient by nature . . . when the case takes a little longer . . ."

The small barkeeper nodded wisely.

"Youth," he said sagely and with infuriating patience. "I gets it. I usta be the same when I were younger. Allays banging me head against the wall. Gots the bumps to show ye." He paused, sipped and took a deep breath. "Speaking of the Baron . . . it's just plain stupid to stiff somebody for no reason. The Baron were a tramp with a past . . . so what . . . there's whole armies like that. Whadda they want with 'im dead?" He cocked his head and winked at DeKok. "They was better off to keep 'im alive."

"You mean in connection with the millionaire?"

"You knows about that?"

"Yes," nodded DeKok, sipping thoughtfully and with obvious relish. "Yes, the Baron and Jack Stuff had figured out a scheme to relieve the millionaire of a lot of money. We know about that. But they weren't in it alone. I mean . . . there was a third man involved. A certain Raymond Verbruggen."

Lowee lifted the bottle and poured refills.

"*Inna Belg*," he said in Flemish, "*d'Anvers*," he added in French and then, mercifully, continued in his usual gutter Dutch: "A real slimer. Most ofta guys don't trust him one bit."

DeKok wondered idly how many bits and pieces of various cultures Lowee had picked up over the years. No doubt he spoke a smattering of at least a dozen languages and DeKok already knew he had more than a passing knowledge of Shakespeare.

"Perhaps he liked the Baron better dead . . . less dangerous."

"Tha's possible . . . bit I ain't heard nuthin about it."

"He deals?"

"Who?"

"Verbruggen."

"Yessir, Big Aitch mostly. It come in onna boat from Marseilles." The last word was pronounced in accent-free French. "*Aitch* is heroin," he added with a condescending nod in Vledder's direction.

"How do you know?" asked DeKok sharply, quickly, before Vledder could respond.

The barkeeper laughed secretively.

"You wanna know about 'im, ain't I right or ain't I right?" It sounded like a challenge.

"I'm interested," said DeKok easily.

"I *knows* it," grinned Lowee, triumph in his voice. "You guys done been chasing 'im for some time." He waved toward the back and made a beckoning gesture. "Ace" Allan stood up and approached the bar.

"You knows Mr. DeKok?"

171

"For ages," answered the old card shark.

"Tell 'em whadda you knows."

Allan grimaced and made a gesture with thumb and forefinger as if counting money.

"What's in it for me?" he asked moodily.

Lowee's face turned red with anger. He leaned closer to the card player.

"*I'll* takes care of that," he spat. "Whadda you think? You thinks I go back on me word? You say I ain't good for it?"

Allan took a step back, shocked by the venom in Lowee's words.

"Tonight," he said reluctantly, "comes the black swan."

DeKok's eyebrows danced across his forehead. All three, Vledder, Allan and Lowee, were momentarily stunned. Then the display stopped as suddenly as it had started and DeKok's words penetrated.

"Who or what is the black swan?"

* * *

"*Black Swan*," read Vledder, "a passenger ship, Panamanian registry. Currently engaged in cruising the Mediterranean. Leaves Amsterdam every fortnight. Last port of call in the Med is Marseilles."

"And that's where they load the heroin," added DeKok.

"Yes," agreed Vledder, switching his attention from his computer screen to his notes. He typed as he read.

"Tonight *Black Swan* will take on a pilot outside Ijmuiden. After a brief delay in the locks she will travel down the North Sea Canal to the West Harbor. Around two a.m. somebody aboard will drop heroine in one kilo bags . . . the bags will be attached to small floats, painted in a light phosphorescent paint. A speed-boat will follow the ship and pick up the floats."

172

"Simplicity itself," grinned DeKok. "It makes all those stories about high-speed chases redundant."

DeKok consulted his watch while Vledder exited his program.

"It's almost nine o'clock. We have more than five hours to take the necessary precautions. We'll inform Chief Inspector Everhard and he can coordinate with the Water Police.'

"And what about us?"

"What do you mean?"

"What are we going to do?"

"About the heroin?"

"Of course!"

"Nothing, absolutely nothing. We'll leave it to Narcotics."

Vledder looked disappointed.

"*They* will get all the credit," he pouted. "And is was *our* tip . . . Lowee is one of our . . . *your* connections."

"I hope," said DeKok virtuously, "that they have a big haul."

Vledder came from behind his desk, highly agitated.

"But we can take care of it. We can contact the Water Police ourselves and than *we* will pick up the heroin and can arrest Verbruggen at the same time."

"I won't even consider it," said DeKok decisively. "How would you like it if Narcotics started to interfere with Homicide?"

He picked up the phone and called Everhard. In short, business-like sentences he relayed the information. He mentioned neither Little Lowee, nor "Ace" Allan.

Vledder, slightly mollified, perched on the edge of DeKok's desk.

"You think Raymond will be in the speed-boat himself?"

"I don't think so." DeKok scratched the tip of his nose. "For the dangerous work he'll no doubt use other personnel, people who'll deliver the stuff to him."

"At Count's Gate?"

"No, that's under surveillance and Verbruggen knows it."

"He knows that?" Vledder sounded surprised.

"Of course he does. You heard what Lowee said. The entire underworld knows that Narcotics has him spotted."

"And yet he takes delivery on another shipment?" Vledder's disbelief was obvious.

"Of course," said DeKok reasonably. "Verbruggen feels safe. While Narcotics keeps Count's Gate under surveillance, he takes delivery . . . at a different address."

"Where?"

"If I knew that . . ." DeKok smiled.

". . . you'd give the info to Everhard," accused Vledder.

"That really bothers you, does it?"

"Well . . ." Vledder blushed. "I would like to ask the elusive Mr. Verbruggen some questions. Not just about drugs."

"About what, pray tell?"

"About everything!" burst out Vledder. "I wouldn't be at all surprised if he was the man behind the murders. It's not at all unthinkable that he was introduced to the millionaire and his wife, using Aunt Aleida, or Abigail, as a go-between. He could also easily have killed Martha. And we *know* he knew the Baron."

DeKok pursed his lips and slowly shook his head.

"It sounds a bit emotional, don't you think? You're not thinking it through. If I didn't know you better, I'd think you were a bit precipitous," he added with mild irony. He paused, shrugged his shoulders. "To tell you the truth, I'm not all that happy about the drug tip, either. It's a surrogate . . . second best."

"I don't understand."

"The last time but one, when we left Lowee's rather abruptly . . . what was then the subject of conversation?"

"The murder of the Baron."

"Exactly," nodded DeKok. "As much as possible, I tried to pressure Lowee into finding out who was responsible for the Baron's death. And Lowee *did* try to find out. I know him well enough for that. He talked to Red Marie, for instance . . . you

174

remember her, Jack Stuff's girlfriend. In an effort to restore his friendly relationship with me, he even promised tip money . . ." His voice trailed away. "And what's the result of all that?" he asked after a while.

"A tip about heroin," answered Vledder superfluously.

"Surrogate . . . second choice." DeKok pressed his lips together, an angry look on his face. Then he went on: "Lowee couldn't discover anything about the Baron's death, but by asking around among his own circle of informants, he stumbled on the information about Raymond Verbruggen and wondered if the police would be interested."

"Yes, I see," nodded Vledder. ". . . and because he was worried about what you thought of him, as a sort of consolation prize, he offered you the valuable information about heroin."

"Valuable is the operative word. You can take it from me, 'Ace' Allan doesn't come cheap."

"How did he get the information?"

DeKok shrugged his shoulders.

"He frequents all the gambling places in the country, illegal, or legal. And his ears are always open."

"Who visits that sort of place?"

"Professional gamblers and people with more money than sense."

"Raymond Verbruggen?"

"Possibly. Gambling houses and casinos are often used as a distribution point for illicit drugs. Therefore it's not all that strange that the tip originated there."

"I bet 'Ace' could tell us a lot more. Shouldn't we have him in?"

"It wouldn't help," disagreed DeKok, "I've known him for some time."

"But surely he knows where he got the information and from whom?"

"Sure he does . . . and so do I: *From some guy on the rear platform of the number seven streetcar.*"

"What!?"

DeKok laughed at Vledder's bewildered expression.

"The only answer you'll get from 'Ace' Allan. It's been his answer for more than twenty years."

Bikerk, The Watch Commander poked his head around the door. He gave a happy grin when he discovered DeKok. He made his way through the desks. He looked pleasantly surprised.

"I thought you'd already left. I was going to leave a note on your desk."

"What sort of note?"

Bikerk looked at his clipboard, covered with numerous pieces of paper, forms and several yellow sheets with closely scribbled notes.

"A message from Dr. Nienhouse."

"From the old Willy?"

"Yes, from the Wilhelmina Hospital," corrected Bikerk punctiliously. "He wants you to contact him."

"What about?"

"A patient . . . Archibald Vanderwehr."

"What's the matter with him?" DeKok's voice was tense.

"He walked away from the hospital," answered Bikerk.

* * *

Inspector DeKok replaced the telephone on its cradle. There was a sober expression on his face and the creases in his forehead were deeper.

"Shortly after Archibald recovered from his coma, he dressed himself and walked away. He shook off a nurse who wanted to stop him. Dr. Nienhouse is very worried. He wanted to know if I had any idea about Vanderwehr's whereabouts because he should be returned to the hospital as soon as possible. His

176

physical condition is still a matter of concern and he will need medical supervision for some time." He sighed a tired sigh. "We have no choice. We *must* find him and quickly. If he dies before we've had a chance to talk to him . . ." He did not complete the sentence, but stared at Vledder without seeing him.

"Where do we begin to look?" asked Vledder.

DeKok scratched the back of his neck.

"First of all, let's call the Blaricum police and ask them to keep an eye on the villa there. I don't think he'll go back there, but we can't ignore the possibility." He walked over to the coat rack and grabbed his decrepit felt hat and disreputable raincoat. "When you're finished, make sure you have a walkie-talkie and join me at Count's Gate." He hesitated, it was the second time in his career that he had advised the use of a personal radio. Then he took the plunge: "And bring your pistol," he added.

Vledder was flabbergasted. Walkie-talkies were one thing, but in all the years he had known DeKok, the old man had never used a firearm and had, on several occasions, dissuaded Vledder from using a weapon. When he recovered from his stunned reaction, he hastened after DeKok. He caught up with him near the door.

"Stop," he panted, "what do you mean? Count's Gate . . . pistol . . . what's happening? Have you lost your mind?" His tone was worried and there was consternation on his face.

DeKok half turned toward him, the doorknob already in his hand.

"Vanderwehr was found there," he muttered. "remember? The bash on his head that knocked him out?" He passed through the door opening, headed for the stairs, wriggling himself into his raincoat. "I think Nephew Archibald has a score to settle." he added over his shoulder.

14

Vledder had caught up. Together they crossed from Inner Bantam Street toward the Old Waal. It rained steadily. The elms along the river seemed depressed by the load of water they retained in their crowns. The river water murmured among the houseboats along the shore, barely perceptible above the constant rush of the rain. DeKok pulled up his collar and pressed his hat further down over his forehead. His brain was in high gear. He sensed that the solution was near and that the last phase had been initiated. He fervently wished for a peaceful end to the case . . . calm, without violence, but he was not at all sanguine about it.

Vledder paced him. The short antenna from the walkie-talkie protruded a few inches above the collar of his trench coat. He was trying to figure out what DeKok expected, but his thoughts drew a blank. He kept silent to hide his ignorance.

Near the end, where the river made a sudden bend, within sight of the Montelbaan Tower, DeKok stopped. Close to the railing of the bridge they saw the red, unmarked car wherein Dijk had assumed his post. The doors were locked and Dijk was nowhere to be seen. DeKok turned away from the car and motioned Vledder closer.

"Call Dijk on your thingamajig."

Vledder placed a hand inside his coat, brought his mouth closer to his collar and made some adjustment.

"Come in, Dijk."

Almost immediately there was a response.

"Dijk here."

DeKok leaned closer to Vledder's chest and spoke. He relied on Vledder to make sure the transmission would be smooth.

"Where are you?"

"Rembrandt Square, near the Arcade."

"What's are you doing there?"

"I'm watching a bar, Berliner Hoff, the two of them went in there."

"When?"

"About half an hour ago."

"Did they go anywhere else?"

"No, they came straight here. I checked, carefully, of course. They come here often."

"Did they contact a man?"

"Not as far I know. Of course, I can't always look inside."

"Well, go inside and have a beer yourself . . . on me. As soon as they start to leave, report. Understood?"

"Understood."

"Don't get help from Half Moon Alley," added Vledder jokingly, while DeKok frowned disapprovingly.

"Dijk out."

Vledder had referred to the police station at Half Moon Alley, near Rembrandt Square. The station is probably the smallest operating police station in the world. It consists of two small rooms, one cell and a bicycle rack. The station is visited by a lot of tourists since it is located halfway between English Pilgrim Alley and the Rembrandt House.

Still shaking his head, DeKok walked over to the abandoned police car and handed the keys to Vledder.

"Where did you get the keys?" asked Vledder as he opened the doors.

"Bikerk gave me the spares."

Vledder seated himself behind the wheel while DeKok got in on the passenger side.

"Where are we going?"

"Nowhere," answered DeKok. "We wait here."

"What for?"

DeKok pointed in the direction of Count's Gate.

"We wait until Everhard withdraws his troops."

"Will he?"

"Oh, yes." DeKok pursed his lips, considering. "*Operation North Sea Canal* isn't all that easy, you know. He's got to cover both shores and there are a number of side canals. In order to cover everything, he'll need a lot of people. And, as he complained, he's chronically short-handed. Even with the help from the Water Police, he'll need every officer he can lay a hand on."

"Is that why you turned it over to him? Because it would take too much personnel?"

DeKok seemed oblivious to both the question and the implication. He slid comfortably down in his seat until his eyes were just able to peek over the edge of the dashboard.

"Turn on the wipers, every once in a while . . . and keep your eyes on that gray van."

"Which one?"

"There, on the other side of the water, almost opposite number thirty-seven, on the edge of the quay."

"Why?"

"That's where they are."

"The Narcotics people?"

"I know Everhard," smiled DeKok. "I know how he works."

They remained silent as the time passed. They could hear the occasional noise of traffic on Prince Henry Quay and they observed a few lone rats scurrying across the bridge in search of who knew what. Rats are an inevitable fact of life in and around the many canals of Amsterdam.

About an hour and a half later DeKok was proved right. The gray van suddenly moved and disappeared in the direction of *Rapenburg* Canal, parallel to Prince Henry Quay and the harbor. DeKok looked at his watch. It was just past midnight. He poked Vledder with an elbow.

"Let's drive across."

"To where the van was?"

"No, park near the old warehouses of the Dutch-West Indian Company. It'll be less noticeable."

Vledder drove slowly toward the indicated place. On the bridge he switched off the engine and free-wheeled the last part toward the warehouses. DeKok emerged from the car and stared up at the facade of number thirty-seven. Vledder joined him. DeKok pulled his hand out of his pocket, Handy Henkie's "lock seducer" between his fingers.

"What do you expect to find?" whispered Vledder.

"Depth."

"What!?"

DeKok had approached the door. His sensitive fingers felt around the lock and within minutes the lock yielded. The lock clicked and the door opened. Cautiously they entered.

The yellow light of DeKok's flashlight reached out down the length of the marble corridor and drew strange shadows from the chubby cherubims on the ceiling. It came back to them from a full-sized mirror in a gilded frame at the end of the corridor. DeKok halted in front of the mirror and surveyed his reflection with a crooked grin on his face. He pushed his hat further back on his head and scratched the back of his neck. After a few seconds he bent down and directed the flashlight at the floor. Then he straightened out and carefully followed the contours of the gilded frame with the beam of light. Vledder followed his actions with interest.

"What about depth?" he asked.

DeKok did not answer. The gilded frame seemed to have absorbed all his attention. His fingertips slid along the edge, searching for a hidden mechanism. Suddenly there was a movement. Frame and mirror pivoted slowly aside. Behind the mirror they discovered an uneven opening, leading to a rough brick corridor.

"A deep house," said DeKok, "I suspected it."

He moved the mirror and played the flashlight over the back of the glass.

"One-way glass," he commented. "Useful. Every visitor can be scrutinized at leisure."

"Where does it lead?" asked Vledder.

"Probably to the house backing up to this one and from there to Pepper Street."

Vledder grinned softly.

"Now I know why the Narcotics people never saw anybody. Raymond went in and out through this secret passage."

"Yes," nodded DeKok, "and it's such a warren behind here, they would have needed a few hundred cops to guard every possible exit and entrance. You see," he continued, "I had a feeling that Raymond hadn't ceased his operations and when 'Ace' told us about the shipment tonight, I was practically certain. While everybody was watching the front, the business was carried on from Pepper Street." He smiled thinly. "Everhard will be surprised as well. I don't think he . . ."

He stopped in mid-sentence. Suddenly Vledder's walkie-talkie had come to life. The young Inspector quickly placed a hand in his coat and pulled the instrument into view.

"Dijk here," they heard.

"Vledder, go ahead."

"They left Berliner Hoff. At this moment they're in Amstel Street, proceeding toward Blue Bridge."

DeKok visualized Blue Bridge, considered Amsterdam's most elegant bridge and an exact replica of the *Pont Alexandre* in

Paris. He looked at his watch and made a quick mental calculation. He motioned toward Vledder, who immediately held the radio closer to DeKok.

"DeKok here. Robert, I think they'll probably walk home via New Owl Fort Street. In that case we'll have another ten or fifteen minutes. If they take a different route, or if they take a cab, report immediately. Understood?"

"Understood."

"Have you seen any man with them?"

"No, should I have?"

DeKok hesitated.

"If something unexpected happens," he said after a brief pause, "don't you hesitate. Call Headquarters and ask for immediate assistance. Understood."

"Understood. Is that all?"

DeKok nodded.

"Yes," answered Vledder. "Out."

"Roger, wilco, over and out," answered the tinny voice of Dijk.

That boy watches too many movies, thought DeKok as Vledder replaced the radio inside his coat.

* * *

Several canals away, Dijk went through the same motions while he watched the beautiful Abigail and her mother across the street. He was diagonally behind them. He allowed the distance to increase slightly without taking his eyes off them.

There were a good many people in the street, despite the late hour. Among them was a young man in a beige corduroy suit. His face looked gray and distorted. Beard stubble sprouted on his chin and cheeks and he shivered in the chilly night air. A drunk bumped into him. Roughly he pushed away the inebriated man. His

184

red-rimmed eyes were glued to the two women who, arm in arm, crossed the Blue Bridge in the direction DeKok had predicted.

* * *

The Inspectors pulled shut the mirror behind them. Carefully, on the tips of their toes, they walked down the rough brick corridor. DeKok's flashlight explored ahead of them. After about thirty yards they reached a closed door.

Again DeKok produced his instrument and the door yielded within seconds. Astonished they stared into a large, wide space. A number of neon lights threw a harsh illumination on a green Citroen DS21. Crates and boxes were stacked along the walls. To the right was a small window. Behind the window they saw a desk, a chair and a telephone.

DeKok pointed at the floor.

"A second car has been parked here."

"Raymond Verbruggen" swallowed Vledder. "Of course he could never use *this* car again."

The gray sleuth put his flashlight away and came out with a pocket knife. He went to one of the crates and loosened the lid. Slowly he lifted it off. Vledder leaned over his shoulder.

"Camel saddles."

DeKok sniffed.

"*Smuggle* saddles," he corrected.

With a powerful stroke he ripped the red leather of the saddle. The sickly sweet smell of pure, uncut hashish rose from the crate. He pulled out part of the saddle padding and pushed it in the pocket of his raincoat. Then he pressed the lid back on the crate and tapped the nails back in place with the handle of his pocket knife. He stole a glance at his watch.

"We better get out of here," he spoke hurriedly. "We haven't got much time left."

They walked past the green car toward the garage doors. DeKok inspected the lock. Suddenly they heard a car on the other side of the door. Brakes screeched and a car door slammed. Hasty footsteps approached.

Both Inspectors retreated from the door and hid behind the boxes. DeKok took a position to the side of the garage doors and Vledder nearly opposite. Vledder pulled out his pistol. The blueblack metal reflected the light from overhead.

The wide doors separated and a man appeared in the opening. DeKok recognized him at once . . . Raymond Verbruggen.

Vledder jumped forward, pistol leveled at the Belgian.

"Police . . . you're under arrest."

The Belgian crouched low to the ground. The movement was incredibly fast. Almost instantaneously a shot rang out. DeKok watched as the pistol fell from Vledder's hand and clattered on the floor.

Raymond Verbruggen straightened up from his crouched position and walked over to Vledder, the pistol which he had carried in an ankle holster in his right hand. There was a cold look in his eyes as he leaned over the helpless Vledder. DeKok took a silent step closer. He was outside Verbruggen's field of vision. Another step . . . one more step and he would be able to raise his fist and hit the Belgian in the neck. DeKok was confident that it would knock the man out. The Belgian had turned Vledder onto his back and now studied the face. A hint of recognition came into his eyes. DeKok was now in position and within a flash Raymond would have been felled by the sledgehammer blow of DeKok's fury.

Suddenly a second shot cracked through the silence and Verbruggen collapsed on top of Vledder's inert body.

DeKok looked foolishly at his own fist. He knew he had not touched the man. So absorbed had he been that it took a moment before he realized that Verbruggen's collapse and the second shot were somehow connected.

He looked around. A pale, young man stood in the opening of the garage doors. A beige, corduroy suit hung around his frame with too much room for the emaciated body. An old service revolver dangled from a shaking hand. A senseless grin disfigured his features.

DeKok at speed was always a comical sight. But this time there was nothing comical about his movements as he kicked Verbruggen's pistol out of reach of the dying man, scooped up Vledder's pistol in almost the same movement and approached Archibald Vanderwehr in two, three steps that seemed to take no time at all. His powerful hand clamped down on the wrist of the swaying young man, forcing him to drop the revolver.

Vanderwehr looked at him with dull eyes, the foolish, vacant grin still on his face.

"He was a swine," he said tonelessly. "They were both swine."

DeKok nodded and led him outside.

Sirens blared in the distance.

15

Laughing happily, one arm in a sling and his other hand encumbered by a bouquet of roses, Vledder looked at DeKok as he opened the door.

"Robert Antoine is here already?"

"Yes," answered his host. "He, too, had roses."

Vledder's face fell. He lifted the bouquet.

"Nicer?" he asked.

"Just as nice," said DeKok diplomatically.

Mrs. DeKok smiled at the young man and was obviously pleased as she accepted the flowers.

"How's your arm?" she asked, concern in her voice.

"Another three, four weeks . . . if all goes well. Then I'll be allowed to go back on duty."

"I'll be happy for my husband. He complains it's no fun without you."

"Did he really say that?" Vledder blushed with pleasure as Mrs. DeKok nodded in confirmation.

Together they entered the cozy living room. Dijk looked like a fashion photograph in a modern, sea-green suit.

Vledder looked at him, appraised him.

"Robert," he asked facetiously, "why did you take the suit after the showing? I didn't think models were allowed to do that."

Mrs. DeKok hastily intervened.

189

"Robert Antoine has taste," she decided in a voice that brooked no argument. She looked disapprovingly at the old pants worn by her husband. "You can't say that about many men," she added.

DeKok grimaced. He liked old, comfortable clothes. Fashion was not one of his concerns.

Vledder found a seat while he watched DeKok carefully warming some brandy snifters over a pale blue flame. He suddenly realized that a similar occasion had arisen at least a dozen times in the last three years. It had become a tradition and he approved.

While DeKok busied himself with the cognac, Mrs. DeKok carried several trays from the kitchen. Dijk jumped up, ready to help but with a motherly smile she waved him back into his chair. She was genuinely fond of the young men who worked with her husband. The food was to be consumed along with the drinks. The Dutch seldom drink just to drink. And they almost never drink without eating. Entire cookbooks are filled with recipes for food to be eaten while drinking. Mrs. DeKok assembled a veritable smorgasbord on a sideboard while DeKok poured the first drinks in the carefully heated glasses. With pride he showed the label of the venerable cognac as his wife presented the drinks to her young guests.

"Chief Inspector Everhard is not such a bad guy, after all," remarked Vledder after they had taken their first delightful sips. "He came to visit me in the hospital and he admitted honestly that he'd made a mistake . . . gave us all the credit."

"It wasn't entirely his fault," commented DeKok as he nestled himself into an easy chair. "*Black Swan* was almost two hours ahead of schedule and he simply lacked the time to get ready. The net was not entirely closed and Verbruggen managed to slip through. He raced down Canal F, near the dumps and before anybody could take action, he had loaded the stuff in his car and was gone."

"To Pepper Street."

190

"Where you expected him to surrender without a struggle," grinned DeKok.

Vledder gestured with his free hand.

"Dammit . . . sorry, ma'am, that guy was so fast. I felt the bullet almost before I realized what he was doing. I never saw the weapon."

Mrs. DeKok looked concerned.

"In retrospect, you were lucky. Just a few centimeters to the right, Dick and we . . ." She did not complete the sentence but gave him a doting smile.

"Happily," said DeKok, "Verbruggen shot too fast, too hurried."

"When I suddenly saw Vanderwehr in the door with that cannon, I really worried. I saw you too, of course, but I seemed unable to move. Everything went in slow motion. I realized that you were concentrating on the Belgian and I wasn't worried about what he could do to me. But I had no idea what Vanderwehr was doing there and no way to warn you." He paused and took a sip from his drink. The emotions from that night returned. His face was pale and his lower lip quivered. "Then Raymond fell on top of me and everything seemed to go blank. It took a while to get it sorted out, but then it was all over."

Robert Antoine leaned forward.

"What has Archibald Vanderwehr . . . I mean, what's his involvement with the case?"

DeKok gestured expansively.

"Everything. He has . . ." He suddenly stopped. The tension left his face and he relaxed. "Come on," he said, lifting the bottle, "first let's eat, drink and be merry. The night is young."

"Why did he kill Verbruggen?" pursued Vledder, watching with satisfaction as the level in his glass rose.

"Because he hated him." said DeKok. "He hated him intensely. He *wanted* to kill him, *needed* to kill him. As far as

191

Vanderwehr was concerned, Verbruggen was a swine. They were both swines."

"Who was the second swine?"

DeKok leaned back, sipped from his drink.

"It's a rather complicated business," he began calmly. "That's probably why it took so long before I started to understand what was happening. All those events . . . all those people . . . it just didn't connect in any way. Perhaps the best thing is to go back to October thirteen of last year."

"The day Manefeldt withdrew money from his bank for the last time," knew Vledder.

"Yes," said DeKok. "It was a large sum, all in cash. We really never wondered what happened to the money . . . why he withdrew it."

"You're right," said Vledder puzzled. "Was it important?"

"It was the direct cause of Manefeldt's death."

"The money?"

"No, the ultimate destination, the purpose of the money." He rocked the glass in his hand and stared at the golden-brown liquid as if trying to find inspiration in its depths.

"I liked Aunt Helen," he continued softly. "It may sound strange, but I felt a certain sympathy for her from the first time I heard her name. She was a sweet, soft and above all, a very religious woman who was able to withstand the humiliations from her tyrannical husband with the strength of her faith. She was helped therein by the trust, loyalty and devotion of Martha Noyes, her friend and confidant." He paused. His tone changed, became hard. "In Antwerp Aleida Drosselhoff and her beautiful daughter, Abigail, came to know a man who was, albeit in a modest way, involved in the illicit drug trade."

"Raymond Verbruggen," grimaced Vledder.

"Exactly. Because things were getting too hot for them in Antwerp, the trio moved to Amsterdam and rented the house at Count's Gate. In order to facilitate his illegal business, Raymond took certain precautions. Under assumed names he rented at least three properties in Pepper Street, he installed the one-way mirror and the secret passage and organized the 'Beauty Consultant' business as a front." He paused and accepted a small plate, heaped with delicacies, from his wife. Carefully he placed the plate next to him on a small table. "Everything went swimmingly," he continued, "but Raymond wasn't satisfied. He wanted more. Everything was still too small, too piece-meal for him. He dreamed about being a real player . . . organizing a syndicate, a widespread trade in drugs with 'King' Verbruggen at its head. But for such grandiose plans he needed money . . . lots of money. He discussed the matter with Aleida . . ."

Vledder stared at him with wide-eyed comprehension.

"And of course she knew somebody . . ." he said, almost choking on a particularly luscious piece of raw herring provided by Mrs. DeKok. ". . . her brother-in-law and ex-lover, the multimillionaire Manefeldt."

"Right, She took Verbruggen to Blaricum and introduced him to the father of her child. Manefeldt was immediately enthusiastic and promised the necessary funds." He placed his glass on the little table and lifted the plate. "Although the conference was held in utmost secrecy, one other person heard everything . . ."

". . . Aunt Helen," guessed Mrs. DeKok.

"Mmmmm," uttered DeKok, his mouth full with a delicious croquette. When he had swallowed the morsel, he said: "Indeed, Aunt Helen." His voice sounded somber. "She realized immediately what the conference was all about and what it would mean. As soon as Manefeldt, a highly intelligent businessman, supported by millions, were to get involved in the drug trade, it would inevitably mean death and misery for thousands and thousands of people. As soon as Aleida and Raymond had left, she tried to persuade her husband to abstain from the drug trade. But Manefeldt refused, abused her physically and verbally. He took the money from the bank and that same day opened an account in the name of Raymond Verbruggen. Aunt Helen was at wit's end. In her despair she turned to the only person in her family she trusted."

"Aha, Nephew Archibald," said Dijk.

"At that time," said DeKok, ignoring the interruption, "the roles had been assigned, the premises defined and everything was ready for the denouement."

"Don't be so melodramatic," chided his wife.

Her husband smiled at her.

"I didn't mean it the way it sounded," he apologized, "on the contrary. It's sad, pitiful. With crime it's the same as with the *Sorcerer's Apprentice*. After the magic words have been said, there's no turning back ... things will happen and the consequences will gain in importance as time progresses. There's no stopping. No matter what the participants might want ... the magic word is missing."

"Shit happens," murmured Vledder *sotto voce*. Mrs. DeKok rolled her eyes at him and smiled. Fortunately, she thought, nobody else had heard him. She knew, better than most, DeKok's opinion about strong language, but she always seemed to be able to forgive the young Inspector his infrequent lapses.

"Very well, Jurriaan," she admonished, covering up for Vledder. "Stick to the facts."

"Nephew Archibald," DeKok went on resignedly, "arrived on the scene in response to a summons from his Aunt Helen. There's a violent argument and young Vanderwehr confessed to being a morphine addict. He wanted to use it as an example, you see. He begs his Uncle to stay away from the drug trade. Manefeldt is more obnoxious than usual and at one point he suggests that the drug business is a good thing, if it means it'll wipe out weaklings like his nephew. Young Archibald lost all self-control, grabbed a heavy candelabra and lashed out. One blow and Uncle Manefeldt is dead."

Meanwhile DeKok had managed to empty the plate his wife had prepared for him. With a satisfied sigh he placed the plate next to him and lifted his glass.

"As soon as they had more or less recovered from the shock," continued DeKok, replacing the empty glass next to the empty plate, "Aunt Helen and her nephew dragged the corpse into the cellar and buried it under a load of coal. Archibald wanted to burn the corpse and argued that the big cooking stove in the kitchen would do the trick. But Aunt Helen was violently opposed. Her religious qualms forbid the cremation of the dead. According to her it's just possible that Our Dear Lord, in his infinite mercy, might just possibly have forgiven her husband his sins. Ergo, Manefeldt is entitled to a Christian burial ... in order to be resurrected according to her beliefs." He lifted the bottle and poured himself another drink. Then he passed the bottle on to Dijk, indicating he should do the honors for those who wanted a refill. Then he went on: "No matter what Nephew Archibald said, Aunt Helen would not be swayed. Her husband was to remain in the cellar."

They fell silent. Dijk seemed stunned, little of this had been in the reports he had seen. Mrs. DeKok, who had heard the story in rough outlines, again felt a wave of pity for the lonely Aunt Helen. Vledder sank back in his chair, since he had not been allowed to read any reports during his convalescence and DeKok had steadfastly refused to discuss the aftermath of the case during his many visits, it was all new to him. In effect Vledder's involvement had ceased when he stopped Verbruggen's bullet. It was for *his* benefit more than anything else, that DeKok reviewed the case at this time.

"Then . . ." ventured Vledder, ". . . young Archibald was *also* responsible for the killing of Martha Noyes."

"Yes. Martha heard from her doctor that she was seriously ill and had but a short time left to live. She's immediately concerned for her invalid sister, Maria. She has to provide for her. She knew all about the murder. Aunt Helen told her. She also knew that young Archibald had inherited a considerable sum from his parent."

"Blackmail? Martha?"

"Needs must when the devil drives," quoted DeKok. "Martha did what she thought necessary. She approached Archibald and, panicked, he paid. She arranged with the attorney she's picked as executor of her estate, to make the necessary arrangements with the nursing home. She's about twenty-five percent short. She went back to Archibald and demanded more money. Vanderwehr promised, but he doesn't *have* the money. When Martha insisted, he saw only one way out . . . murder. It doesn't take a genius to find out her habits. He soon learns about her weekly visits to Hilversum. He steals a car, hits her and that's it. In Holland it is, of course, very easy to get rid of a car in a convenient river, stream or canal. Eventually it will be found, of course, but that can take years." He paused and raked his fingers through his hair. "As it happens, Archibald was too late. Martha had sold the secret to Aunt Aleida."

Vledder sat up.

"So Aunt Aleida knew . . ."

". . . that Archibald had killed his uncle," completed DeKok.

"But why didn't she go to the police?" Dijk wanted to know.

"No proof. She only had a rather incoherent story from Martha. Hear-say, really. She knew full well she would need proof positive before she could approach the police with a convincing story. You must remember that Manefeldt was an eccentric. People in Blaricum were used to him disappearing from time to time. But she did try . . ."

"How do you mean?"

"She did try to find proof, I mean," explained DeKok. "She spent days at the villa, searching, looking into things. Eventually she found Manefeldt's passport and other papers. This find *and* the violent death of Martha, convinced her that her brother-in-law was dead."

"She could have gone to the police, then," suggested Vledder.

"Perhaps. But Aleida Drosselhoff is a schemer, a woman who likes to solve her own problems. One day she summoned Nephew Archibald to Count's Gate. During a friendly little chat she suddenly tells him that she knows he killed his uncle and that he's responsible for the death of Martha Noyes. She gives him a choice . . . produce the corpse, or accompany her to the police."

"But what was the purpose of that? It makes no sense," objected Dijk.

"Of course it did," grinned DeKok. "Aunt Aleida had no interest in a conviction for murder. She couldn't have cared less about that, or about either one of the Archibalds. But she *did* want to make sure that Manefeldt was declared legally dead."

"Legally dead?" Mrs. DeKok looked confused.

"Yes, dear. Aleida knew all about Manefeldt's Last Will and Testament. She even had a copy. She knew that Abigail was the sole beneficiary of the will. She didn't mind at all that the millionaire was dead . . . on the contrary. But his death *must* be recorded and he had to be *legally* dead."

"Otherwise dear Abbie couldn't inherit," mocked Vledder.

"Precisely."

"So," asked Mrs. DeKok, "what was Nephew's reply?"

DeKok raised both arms in protest.

"Before I go on, I need another drink and a few of these little things there." He pointed at the sideboard.

"You can wait," said his wife decisively. The others supported her.

"Very well. Nephew Archibald lied. He said that it was impossible to produce the corpse of his uncle. The body had been burned, he said, and the ashes had been spread over the heather. He would be happy to accompany his aunt to the police, but she

197

shouldn't expect him to confess to murder. He might be dumb, he added, but he wasn't crazy."

"Checkmate," laughed Dijk.

"But not for long," DeKok said grimly. "In April of that year, Jack Stuff visited Count's Gate and bought an ounce of hashish. Jantje is, was, a regular user. He usually came by himself, but this time he's accompanied by a friend, who's anxious to learn all about the drug trade."

"The Baron!"

DeKok nodded at Vledder.

"Aunt Aleida happened to be on guard behind the mirror and immediately noticed the striking resemblance between the Baron and her ex-lover. In a flash she also saw the possibilities."

DeKok picked up the bottle himself, having reached over and removed it from the table next to Dijk. Carefully and with total attention, he poured himself another glass of cognac. He held up the bottle, inviting the others with his eyes. Vledder shook his head, but Dijk happily accepted another drink.

"Go on," urged Vledder as DeKok appeared content to sit and savor the cognac.

"Aunt Aleida," resumed the gray sleuth, "discussed her idea with Verbruggen and they agreed. The only person able to betray the pseudo-Manefeldt is Nephew Archibald and he wouldn't dare to speak out. Carefully she pumped Jack Stuff for information about his friend. Slowly the plan takes shape and by the beginning of May all details have been worked out and they're ready to proceed."

"What went wrong?" asked Vledder. "Why did they change their plans?"

"*They* didn't change their plans," DeKok said mysteriously. Before anybody could protest, he continued: "The night before the big day, Jantje went to visit his friend in the abandoned warehouse he shared with Big Pierre. Big Pierre received him at the door. Jack asked for the Baron and Big Pierre took him to the wall of South

Church. Stunned, Jantje Brewer discovers the corpse of his friend, the Baron. In panic he runs to Count's Gate and tells them that everything is off . . . his friend has passed on. Then he runs back to the corpse and takes away the wallet and papers in an attempt to avoid any possible guilt being attributed to the Baron. Jantje knew that if the papers were found on the corpse the possibility existed that his friend would posthumously be accused of fraud, or conspiracy to defraud. Jantje wanted to spare him that. The next evening Jack is arrested. He's not himself, the death of the Baron has affected him severely. When he learned that the Baron has been murdered with a needle and I accused him of murder, he'd had enough. It was the straw that broke the camel's back."

"He committed suicide," sighed Vledder.

For a long time they remained silent. DeKok was much troubled. He would always feel partly responsible for Jantje's death. Dijk finally broke the silence.

"But Aunt Aleida didn't give up," he said.

DeKok shook his head.

"No, she just waited. The police, so she thought, would find Manefeldt's papers on the corpse and come to the obvious conclusion. She would readily identify the corpse and she would have obtained her objective. Dead or alive, the Baron would accomplish his mission . . . Much to her surprise she read in the paper that the corpse of an 'unknown' had been found. She wasted no time."

Vledder looked grim.

"She sent beautiful Abigail to identify the corpse of her uncle."

"Yes," agreed DeKok. "It was a shrewd move, almost without risks. After all, the two men looked alike and the condition of the corpse could explain any small discrepancies. But the plan went wrong because of two factors, both of them unknown to her: She did not know that the Baron had been murdered and she also did not know that Ferdinand Ferkades, for sentimental reasons, had retained an old photograph of his first wife. And that photo was my first clue that there was something wrong about the identity of the corpse."

"Who tried to kill Vanderwehr?" asked Vledder.

"Nobody," grinned DeKok. "Young Archibald knew that Verbruggen had a green DS21 . . ."

"He was just trying to direct our attention to the Belgian," understood Vledder. He smiled ruefully. "For a moment there, just before I got shot, I actually believed that Verbruggen had *two* identical cars. One in the secret garage, the murder car, and one he used regularly."

"It was an obvious mistake to make, at the time," assured DeKok. "Remember, we were trying to investigate him very carefully and then were called off by Narcotics. No doubt we would eventually have discovered that his other car was that red thing . . . Alpha Beta something."

"Alfa Romeo," corrected Vledder with a smile.

"Whatever," answered DeKok carelessly. "Anyway *that* car was registered to Abigail."

"But what about Vanderwehr?" persisted Dijk.

"When he was unable to make us concentrate on Verbruggen, not knowing that we had been called off by Narcotics, he gave up. Young Archibald isn't nearly as cool and calculating as his aunt. Remember, initially he paid Martha without a struggle . . . Anyway, when she also blocked his move with the imitation Manefeldt, he should have just burned the corpse and cut his losses. But he remembered his promise to Aunt Helen and he gave his uncle a Christian burial . . . under the terrace. He knew, of course, that sooner or later I would return to the villa. Although he didn't say so, I'm almost sure that was part of the reason for moving the corpse out of the cellar."

"He *wanted* to be discovered," said Dijk.

DeKok nodded.

"As I said, he had given up the fight. But he was determined not to go down by himself. Aunt Aleida was to be dragged down with him. Aunt Aleida and another . . . Raymond Verbruggen. He blamed Verbruggen primarily for his own addiction to drugs. That's why he wanted him dead."

Again there was a long silence. Mrs. DeKok offered her trays with delicacies and the bottle went round once more. Then Mrs. DeKok disappeared in the kitchen to make coffee.

When she returned, the conversation became more general. The bizarre murders receded into the background and more cheerful subjects were discussed. It was well past midnight when DeKok said goodbye to his visitors. He waved after them as they walked down the street toward their respective homes.

When he returned to the living room, his wife gave him a searching look. DeKok knew that look.

"What is it?" he evaded.

She walked over to him and removed an invisible piece of lint from his collar. She took him by the arm and led him back to his chair. She sat down next to him, holding his hand between hers.

"Nobody asked," she said innocently, "but who killed the Baron?"

DeKok rubbed the bridge of his nose with a little finger and smiled sadly. He reached for his jacket on the back of his chair and produced a yellow, wrinkled paper napkin. He opened it up and held it up against the light. The paper was covered with spidery scribbles.

"What is it?" asked his wife.

DeKok released the piece of paper and watched it flutter to the floor.

"Another stupidity of Big Pierre."

"Big Pierre?"

"Yes," nodded DeKok pensively. "Big Pierre, the man who was so jealous of Jack Stuff's friendship with the Baron that he couldn't stand it. He felt left out, wanted to keep the Baron for himself . . . didn't want to share him. We were so concerned with the drugs and with what had happened to Manefeldt, we almost forgot about the Baron's killer. But it was Pierre."

"*He* gave the injection?"

DeKok did not look at her.

"While the Baron was asleep, secure in the abandoned warehouse they shared, Pierre gave the fatal injection. He then dressed his dead friend and placed him against the church wall. In order to put the blame on young Archibald, he hid the hypodermic in the villa. But he forgot two things . . . in the first place Vanderwehr *never* used opium and secondly, Pierre left his fingerprints all over the hypodermic."

Mrs. DeKok pointed at the paper napkin on the floor.

"Did he write that?"

"Yes, a confession."

"And?"

"Big Pierre . . . was arrested this morning."

About the Author:

Albert Cornelis Baantjer (BAANTJER) first appeared on the American literary scene in September, 1992 with "DeKok and Murder on the Menu". He was a member of the Amsterdam Municipal Police force for more than 38 years and for more than 25 years he worked Homicide out of the ancient police station at 48 Warmoes Street, on the edge of Amsterdam's Red Light District. The average tenure of an officer in "the busiest police station of Europe" is about five years. Baantjer stayed until his retirement.

His appeal in the United States has been instantaneous and praise for his work has been universal. "If there could be another Maigret-like police detective, he might well be Detective-Inspector DeKok of the Amsterdam police," according to *Bruce Cassiday* of the International Association of Crime Writers. "It's easy to understand the appeal of Amsterdam police detective DeKok," writes *Charles Solomon* of the Los Angeles Times. Baantjer has been described as "a Dutch Conan Doyle" (Publishers Weekly) and has been called "a new major voice in crime fiction in America" (*Ray B. Browne*, CLUES: A Journal of Detection).

Perhaps part of the appeal is because much of Baantjer's fiction is based on real-life (or death) situations encountered during his long police career. He writes with the authority of an expert and with the compassion of a person who has seen too much suffering. He's been there.

The critics and the public have been quick to appreciate the charm and the allure of Baantjer's work. Seven "DeKok's" have been used by the (Dutch) Reader's Digest in their series of condensed books (called "Best Books" in Holland). In his native Holland, with a population of less than 15 million people, Baantjer has sold more than 4 million books and according to the Netherlands Library Information Service, a Baantjer/DeKok is checked out of a library more than 700,000 times per year.

A sampling of American reviews suggests that Baantjer may become as popular in English as he is already in Dutch.

Murder in Amsterdam
Baantjer

The two very first "DeKok" stories for the first time in a single volume, containing *DeKok and the Sunday Strangler* and *DeKok and the Corpse on Christmas Eve*.

First American edition of these European
Best-Sellers in a single volume.

ISBN 1 881164 00 4

From critical reviews of **Murder in Amsterdam**:

If there could be another Maigret-like police detective, he might well be Detective-Inspector DeKok of the Amsterdam police. Similarities to Simenon abound in any critical judgement of Baantjer's work (*Bruce Cassiday*, **International Association of Crime Writers**); The two novellas make an irresistible case for the popularity of the Dutch author. DeKok's maverick personality certainly makes him a compassionate judge of other outsiders and an astute analyst of antisocial behavior (*Marilyn Stasio*, **The New York Times Book Review**); Both stories are very easy to take (**Kirkus Reviews**); Inspector DeKok is part Columbo, part Clouseau, part genius, and part imp. Baantjer has managed to create a figure hapless and honorable, bozoesque and brilliant, but most importantly, a body for whom the reader finds compassion (*Steven Rosen*, **West Coast Review of Books**); Readers of this book will understand why the author is so popular in Holland. His DeKok is a complex, fascinating individual (*Ray Browne*, **CLUES: A Journal of Detection**); This first translation of Baantjer's work into English supports the mystery writer's reputation in his native Holland as a Dutch Conan Doyle. His knowledge of esoterica rivals that of Holmes, but Baantjer wisely uses such trivia infrequently, his main interests clearly being detective work, characterization and moral complexity (**Publishers Weekly**);

DeKok and the Somber Nude
Baantjer

The oldest of the four men turned to DeKok: "You're from
Homicide?" DeKok nodded. The man wiped the raindrops from
his face, bent down and carefully lifted a corner of the canvas.
Slowly the head became visible: a severed girl's head. DeKok
felt the blood drain from his face. "Is that all you found?" he
asked. "A little further," the man answered sadly, "is the rest."
Spread out among the dirt and the refuse were the remaining
parts of the body: both arms, the long, slender legs, the petite
torso. There was no clothing.

First American edition of this European Best-Seller.

ISBN 1 881164 01 2

From critical reviews of **DeKok and the Somber Nude**:

It's easy to understand the appeal of Amsterdam police detective
DeKok; he hides his intelligence behind a phlegmatic demeanor,
like an old dog that lazes by the fireplace and only shows his
teeth when the house is threatened (*Charles Solomon*, **Los Angeles Times**); A complete success. Like most of Baantjer's stories,
this one is convoluted and complex (**CLUES: A Journal of Detection**); Baantjer's laconic, rapid-fire storytelling has spun out a
surprisingly complex web of mysteries (**Kirkus Reviews**);

DeKok and the Dead Harlequin
Baantjer

Murder, double murder, is committed in a well-known Amsterdam hotel. During a nightly conversation with the murderer DeKok tries everything possible to prevent the murderer from giving himself up to the police. Risking the anger of superiors DeKok disappears in order to prevent the perpetrator from being found. But he is found, thanks to a six-year old girl who causes untold misery for her family by refusing to sleep. A respected citizen, head of an important Accounting Office is deadly serious when he asks for information from the police. He is planning to commit murder. He decides that DeKok, as an expert, is the best possible source to teach him how to commit the perfect crime.

First American edition of this European Best-Seller.

ISBN 1 881164 04 7

From critical reviews of **DeKok and the Dead Harlequin**:

Baantjer's latest mystery finds his hero in fine form. As in Baantjer's earlier works, the issue of moral ambiguity once again plays heavily as DeKok ultimately solves the crimes (**Publishers Weekly**); . . . real clarity and a lot of emotional flexibility (**Scott Meredith Literary Agency**); DeKok has sympathy for the human plight and expresses it eloquently (*Dr. R.B. Browne*, **Bowling Green State University**).

DeKok and the Sorrowing Tomcat
Baantjer

Peter Geffel (Cunning Pete) had to come to a bad end. Even his Mother thought so. Still young, he dies a violent death. Somewhere in the sand dunes that help protect the low lands of the Netherlands he is found by an early jogger, a dagger protruding from his back. The local police cannot find a clue. They inform other jurisdictions via the police telex. In the normal course of events, DeKok (Homicide) receives a copy of the notification. It is the start of a new adventure for DeKok and his inseparable sidekick, Vledder. Baantjer relates the events in his usual, laconic manner and along the way he reveals unexpected insights and fascinating glimpses of the Netherlands.

First American edition of this European Best-Seller.

ISBN 1 881164 05 5

From critical reviews of **DeKok and the Sorrowing Tomcat**:

The pages turn easily and DeKok's offbeat personality keeps readers interested (**Publishers Weekly**). Baantjer is at his very best. There's no better way to spend a hot or a cold day than with this man who radiates pleasure, adventure and overall enjoyment. A ***** rating for this author and this book (**CLUES: A Journal of Detection**).

Also available in hard-cover (bound)

ISBN 1 881164 61 6

DeKok and the Dancing Death
Baantjer

A tall girl, dressed in a multi-colored skirt, an open blouse and long, black hair asks DeKok for a final resting place for her girl friend, Colette. Colette has died of an overdose and has been dead for two days. The body is "stored" in an abandoned building. It is the first in a series of questions that keep DeKok occupied for some time. The questions lead to unexpected answers. It starts with a small, blond boy, found in a cardboard box, next to the dead girl. It leads, via blackmail and addiction, to murder. DeKok's greatest concern is for the child, who he hopes to spare from the fate of his mother.

First American edition of this European Best-Seller.

ISBN 1 881164 11 X

DeKok and the Naked Lady
Baantjer

This is the twelfth book about DeKok and his assistant, Vledder. This time it also means an even dozen murders. The victims of a systematic murderer are all killed in the same way. *Shutto gammen-uschi* is the name of the karate combination that takes their lives. But that is only the beginning of the puzzle. It starts on a sunny morning. An eight-year old boy delivers a notification of death to DeKok. "At the request of the deceased, no crocuses, or other flowers." When DeKok and Vledder return to their car, after the funeral, they find a card under the windshield wiper: "Ask for the naked lady ..." Karate, divorces, sex theaters, crocuses and twelve serial killings. In this labyrinth of facts, where witnesses contradict each other, only DeKok knows the exit.

First American edition of this European Best-Seller.

ISBN 1 881164 12 8

DeKok and Murder on the Menu
Baantjer

On the back of a menu from the Amsterdam Hotel-Restaurant *De Poort van Eden* (Eden's Gate) is found the complete, signed confession of a murder. The perpetrator confesses to the killing of a named blackmailer. Inspector DeKok (Amsterdam Municipal Police, Homicide) and his assistant, Vledder, gain possession of the menu. They remember the unsolved murder of a man whose corpse, with three bullet holes in the chest, was found floating in the waters of the Prince's Canal. A year-old case which was almost immediately turned over to the Narcotics Division. At the time it was considered to be just one more gang-related incident. DeKok and Vledder follow the trail of the menu and soon more victims are found and DeKok and Vledder are in deadly danger themselves. Although the murder was committed in Amsterdam, the case brings them to Rotterdam and other, well-known Dutch cities such as Edam and Maastricht.

First American edition of this European Best-Seller.

ISBN 1 881164 31 4

From critical reviews of **DeKok and Murder on the Menu**:

One of the most successful achievements. DeKok has an excellent sense of humor and grim irony (**CLUES: A Journal of Detection**); Terrific on-duty scenes and dialogue, realistic detective work and the allure of Netherlands locations (**The Book Reader**).